007

D0916650

eki kawahara   abec   bee-pee

SWORD ART ONLINE

MOTHER'S ROSARY

"...Mya..."

Kirito § The Black Swordsman, who saved everyone trapped inside *SAO*, the infamous Game of Death. His real name is Kazuto Kirigaya. In *ALO*, he plays a spriggan.

"Uh...aah...I'm sleepy."

Silica § A girl Kirito saved in *SAO*. In *ALO*, she plays a beast-taming cait sith character.

"You can't help but get sleepy, watching him...I wonder if it's one of those illusion magic things that spriggans do."

Lisbeth § A girl who upgraded Kirito's swords in *SAO*. In *ALO*, she is a leprechaun blacksmith.

"...Oh...I see."

Asuna § Kirito's girlfriend. In *ALO*, she plays an undine magician.

"I'm pretty sure the culprit for Silica's sleepiness is over there."

Leafa § Kirito's little sister. Real name: Suguha. She plays a magic fighter sylph in *ALO*.

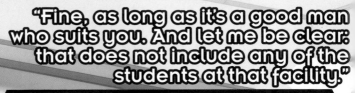

"Fine, as long as it's a good man who suits you. And let me be clear: that does not include any of the students at that facility."

Kyouko Yuuki § Asuna's mother. A college professor heavily invested in her children's education. She wants to transfer Asuna out of the high school she attends with Kazuto.

"Did you...look into him...?"

Asuna Yuuki § Daughter of Shouzou Yuuki, CEO of the major electronics manufacturer RCT. She was trapped inside *Sword Art Online* when she played the copy her brother Kouichirou bought.

Tecchi § A gnome man.

**"What do you say?
Will you accept the
Sleeping Knights' offer?"**

Siune § An undine woman, member of the Sleeping Knights, the Absolute Sword's guild.

Talken § A young leprechaun man.

Jun § A young salamander man.

Nori § A spriggan woman.

"It's finally time!
Let's do our best, Asuna!"

Yuuki § A girl in *ALO* who befriends Asuna after her encounter with the "Absolute Sword." She invites the renowned fencer to join her guild.

Officially known as "Original Sword Skills" (OSS). For the various kinds of weapons that were implemented into *ALfheim Online*, this is a new system of attacking. It's an updated version of the Sword Skills from the old *Sword Art Online*.

The difference between OSS and the former *SAO*'s Sword Skill tree is that, rather than basing everything on the ability to hit predetermined stances and motions, the player himself can create and register his own skills. However, because the system demands that players achieve their combos at physically impossible speeds without any system assistance (a paradoxically difficult task), only a handful of players have ever succeeded in creating and utilizing their own OSS.

However, the Original Sword Skill system has a feature called "skill inheritance." Those who have successfully created a skill can fashion a single-generation copy of that skill in the form of a "Skill Tome," which allows another player to learn and use that OSS. Because creating an OSS is so difficult, these Skill Tomes are among the priciest and rarest of items in *ALO*—particularly the Tomes for combos that include over five hits.

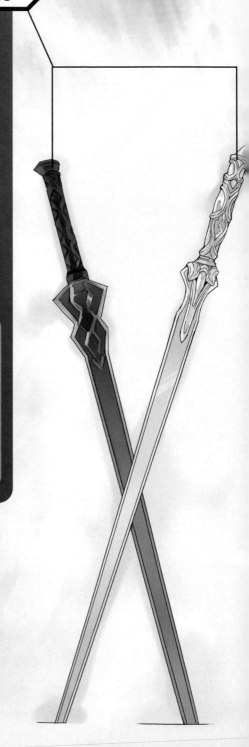

SWORD ART ONLINE
MOTHER'S ROSARY

VOLUME 7

Reki Kawahara

abec

bee-pee

YEN ON

NEW YORK

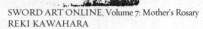

SWORD ART ONLINE, Volume 7: Mother's Rosary
REKI KAWAHARA

Translation by Stephen Paul

SWORD ART ONLINE
©REKI KAWAHARA 2011
All rights reserved.
First published in Japan in 2011 by
KADOKAWA CORPORATION, Tokyo.
English translation rights arranged with
KADOKAWA CORPORATION, Tokyo,
through Tuttle-Mori Agency, Inc., Tokyo.

English translation © 2016 by Yen Press, LLC

Yen On
1290 Avenue of the Americas
New York, NY 10104
www.yenpress.com

Yen On is an imprint of Yen Press, LLC.
The Yen On name and logo are trademarks of Yen Press, LLC.

The publisher is not responsible for websites (or their content) that are not owned by the publisher.

First Yen On edition: April 2016

Library of Congress Cataloging-in-Publication Data

Names: Kawahara, Reki, author. | Abec, 1985- illustrator. | Paul, Stephen
    (Translator) translator.
Title: Sword art online. Volume 7, Mother's rosary / Reki Kawahara ;
    illustration by abec ; translation, Stephen Paul.
Other titles: Mother's rosary
Description: First Yen On edition. | New York, NY : Yen On, 2016. | Series:
    Sword art online ; 7 | Summary: "Kirito and Sinon's battle with Death Gun
    is over, but something strange is afoot in the next-generation VRMMO
    ALfheim Online. A new duelist with a custom sword skill is defeating all
    comers—including Kirito! But when Asuna goes to face this duelist, she
    receives something she never expected: An invitation to an exclusive
    guild!"—Provided by publisher.
Identifiers: LCCN 2015049265 | ISBN 9780316390408 (paperback)
Subjects: | CYAC: Fantasy games—Fiction. | Virtual reality—Fiction. |
    Internet games—Fiction. | Science fiction. | BISAC: FICTION / Science
    Fiction / Adventure.
Classification: LCC PZ7.K1755 Swj 2016 | DDC [Fic]—dc23 LC record available at
http://lccn.loc.gov/2015049265

10 9 8 7 6 5 4 3

LSC-C

Printed in the United States of America

"THIS MIGHT BE A GAME, BUT IT'S NOT SOMETHING YOU PLAY."

—Akihiko Kayaba, *Sword Art Online* programmer

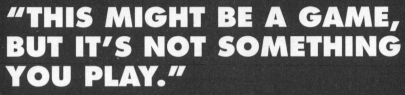

SWORD ART ONLINE
MOTHER'S ROSARY

Reki Kawahara

abec

bee-pee

"Have you heard about the Absolute Sword, Asuna?"

Asuna stopped typing on the holo-keyboard and looked up at Lisbeth.

"Athletic Horde? Are they going to hold a race or something?"

"No, no, no." Lisbeth laughed, shaking her head. She picked up the steaming mug on the table and took a sip. "Clean your ears out. I said *Absolute Sword*."

"Absolute...Sword. Is it a new legendary item they added or something?"

"*Non, non.* It's a person's name. Or...nickname, I guess. A title. I don't know the actual avatar name. Whoever it is, they're so strong that someone started calling them the 'Absolute Sword,' and the name stuck. 'The sword of absolute invincibility,' 'the sword of absolute power'...I think that's what they mean by it."

The moment she heard the word *strong*, Asuna sensed that her curiosity had been tickled.

She knew more than a bit about using a sword. In *ALfheim Online*, she played an undine, who typically stayed back to cast spells in battle, but every now and then she felt the itch to fight again and would pull out her rapier and charge into the enemy's midst. Thanks to that, she was now the unhappy owner of the

"Berserk Healer" nickname, a far cry from the elegance she normally tried to project.

She actively participated in the monthly dueling tournaments to help her master the three-dimensional combat of *ALO*, and she could go toe-to-toe with mighty warriors like the salamandic general Eugene and the sylphic lady Sakuya. News of a brand-new rival could not be overlooked.

Asuna saved her in-progress biology report and banished the holo-keyboard, picking up her own mug and refilling it with the click of a finger. She repositioned herself in her tree-branch seat, satisfied that she was in a comfortable pose for chatting.

"And...? What is this 'Absolute Sword' like?"

"Well..."

1

On the twenty-second floor of New Aincrad, white snow fell upon a deep forest.

In the real world, too, it was the midwinter chill of early January, but with the advancing pace of global warming, Tokyo hardly ever dropped below freezing.

The game management wanted to make the most of the season, however, so Alfheim, realm of fairies, was locked in a devastating winter. North of the World Tree located at the center of the map, it was common for temperatures to fall into the single digits and peak below zero. Nobody wanted to fly in conditions like that without proper equipment or anti-cold buffing spells. At the moment, Aincrad was floating above gnome territory, the northernmost of all the races, and the air was cold enough to cause ice crystals throughout all of its floors.

But even a chill that could freeze a running brook solid could not penetrate the warming effects of thick log walls and a burning-red furnace.

It was eight months since May 2025, when the largest update *ALfheim Online* had ever seen added the massive New Aincrad map to the game.

Because *ALO* functioned on a replica of the system that the formerly deadly *Sword Art Online* ran on, the server already contained all of the data for *SAO*'s setting, the floating castle Aincrad. The new venture that had bought all the rights to *ALO* hardware and software from RCT Progress—its previous administrators—decided on the bold move of preserving all the old *SAO* character data that came along with *ALO*'s back end and, even further, merging it into the game.

Naturally, part of this was a cold, practical decision to shore up their user-base numbers from dropping off after the discovery of RCT Progress's criminal human experiments by offering a massive and exciting new update. But that wasn't the only factor. The investors who put together the new company were all veteran MMO players since the 2-D days, and they couldn't stand to have that meticulously designed world erased forever. At least, that was what Asuna heard from Agil, who served as a pipeline to the administrators.

Since the revival of Aincrad, Asuna had continued through the game as an undine healer/fencer, but with a secret desire in mind.

Naturally, her goal was to raise the necessary col (or wait, it was yrd now) and reach the twenty-second floor before anyone else so she could purchase the little log cabin hidden deep within the pine forest there. It was the very place where, long ago, she had once spent two wonderful, blissful, heartbreaking weeks.

In last May's update, they'd only added the first ten floors. In September they opened eleven through twenty. Then, on Christmas Eve, the night of December 24th, the labyrinth door that led to the twenty-first floor opened. At the moment the little fanfare played to celebrate the unlocking of the new content, Asuna was already racing up the long stairs with a party she'd put together of Kirito, Klein, Agil, Lisbeth, Silica, and Leafa.

The twenty-second floor was a quiet one, almost entirely covered in forest, and there was a number of player homes that could be bought in the main village, so it was unlikely that any rivals were gunning for the same house that she was. But Asuna raced through the twenty-first floor like a tornado anyway, challenged the floor boss in the labyrinth with a joint raid party, and stood at the front of the nearly fifty-man army with her sword, despite being a half-healer build. Afterward, Klein told her that she was "even more impressive than when she was vice commander of the Knights of the Blood."

When she had at last kicked aside the body of the twenty-first-floor boss she'd finished off herself, Asuna raced to the edge of the twenty-second floor where the little cabin waited, hit the OKAY button on the purchasing window, and collapsed in front of it, shedding tears. That night, after all their friends had left the party, she shared a toast with Kirito and their "daughter" Yui, who was back in her human little-girl form, and Asuna bawled again. This time, it was a secret from her friends.

Even Asuna couldn't exactly put into words her fixation on this particular log house. It was the place where she was finally united with the first boy she'd ever truly loved, after a great number of trials and tribulations—virtual or not—and they'd spent a brief but wonderful time together. That was an easy enough explanation, but Asuna felt there was more to it than that.

She had always sought her place in the real world, and perhaps this was her "home" in the truest sense of the word. A comfortable, warm place where a pair of birds could rest their wings and huddle together to sleep. The home of her heart.

Of course, after all the trouble she went through to get it this time around, the log cabin ended up as a hangout spot for their friends, and not a day went by where there wasn't a visitor. Apparently, after her meticulous interior renovation, the house was such a comfortable destination that people would fly up from the surface to visit it. Both her old companions from *SAO* and her new friends in *ALO* would stop by incessantly to smack their lips at her home cooking. There was even one time when, through an act of considerable coincidence, they had a very tense meal with both Lady Sakuya and General Eugene at the table.

On this day—January 6th, 2026—the living-wood stump table in the cabin's main room was surrounded by familiar faces.

To Asuna's right was the beast tamer Silica, sporting the cait sith's signature triangular ears. She was glaring at math equations from her winter vacation homework on a holo-display and groaning. To Asuna's left was Leafa the warrior-mage sylph, her greenish-yellow hair tied into a long ponytail. Like Silica, she was grunting over homework—in this case, an English essay.

Seated across from her was the leprechaun blacksmith Lisbeth, but she was reclined back in the chair with her legs crossed, a bottle of raspberry liquor in one hand and an in-game novel in the other.

In the real world it was around four o'clock, but the time of day in ALfheim wasn't coordinated with the outside world, so it was already after sunset, and the only thing to be seen out of the window was the falling snow catching the light of the lanterns. They didn't need to hear the rustling outside to know that it was freezing cold, but the logs in the stove crackled merrily, and the mushroom stew in the deep pot bubbled and filled the room with warmth and aroma.

Like her friends, Asuna had a holo-keyboard under her hands, poring over a browser window connected to the Internet and working on a school report.

Asuna's mother did not entirely approve of doing tasks in the VR world that could easily be accomplished in reality, but lengthy typing sessions were actually much more efficient here. There was no eye or wrist strain, and she could call up more pages than her actual 1600x1200 monitor could support and place them wherever she wanted.

In an attempt to convince her mother, Asuna once had her log in to a full-dive application meant to facilitate text entry, but within a few minutes, her mother had logged out, complaining that it made her dizzy. She never bothered with it again.

Full-dive sickness was a real thing, but after *living* in that environment for two years, Asuna couldn't even remember what it felt like. Her fingers flashed and flew with perfect accuracy as she approached the conclusion of her report within the editing software.

Just then, something settled on her shoulder.

She turned to the right to see Silica's head resting on her, the large triangular ears twitching as she slept with a satisfied smile.

Asuna couldn't help but grin. She tickled a feline ear with her index finger. "Come on, Silica. If you take a nap now, you'll have trouble falling asleep tonight."

"*Hrm...mya...*"

"There's only three days of vacation left. Better get working on that assignment."

She pulled the ear, causing Silica to twitch and straighten up at last. She stared blearily and blinked several times before shaking her head and looking at Asuna.

"Uh...aah...I'm sleepy," she murmured, and yawned widely, little white fangs visible. The other cait sith players who visited the cabin exhibited similar sleepiness, which made Asuna wonder if there was some kind of racial status effect it had on them.

Asuna looked at Silica's holo-window and said, "You're almost done with that page. Why don't you just breeze through that one?"

"Mmm...hokay..."

"Is it too warm in here? Should I lower the heat?" Asuna asked.

To her left, Leafa giggled. "No, I'm pretty sure the culprit is over there."

"Over there...?"

Asuna, ponytail waving, followed the line of Leafa's finger toward the stove affixed to the eastern wall.

"...Oh...I see," she murmured, nodding. Plopped in front of the red, burning stove was a finely polished wooden rocking chair.

Slumped in the rocking chair and fast asleep was a spriggan boy with tanned skin and short black hair. His formerly spiky hair had been altered to lie flat, but the pointed and mischievous facial features were still intact. It was, of course, Kirito.

A little dragon with pale blue feathers was curled into a ball on his stomach, its head resting comfortably on its soft, curled tail. This was Pina, Silica's miniature dragon partner since the days of *SAO*.

And snoozing on top of Pina's soft down was an even smaller fairy with straight, lustrous black hair and a light-pink one-piece dress. It was Yui, an AI born from the old *SAO* server, now serving as Kirito's navigation pixie. But most important, she was the daughter of Asuna and Kirito.

The three-layer stack of Kirito, Pina, and Yui, each sleeping blissfully on the rocking chair, was having a nearly sorcerous effect on anyone around it. Just watching them for a few seconds was making Asuna's eyelids grow heavy with sleep.

Kirito was quite an avid sleeper himself. As if he was trying to make up for all the sleep he lost trying to defeat *SAO* the first time, Kirito collapsed into his favorite rocking chair and dozed away any time Asuna took her eyes off of him for more than a few moments.

And Asuna did not know anything that made her sleepy faster than the sight of Kirito snoozing in his rocking chair.

When they lived in the old Aincrad and Kirito fell asleep on the couches in the upstairs of Agil's shop or on the porch of their forest cabin, Asuna would almost always slip in next to him and share in the warmth of sleep. She knew from personal experience what a soporific effect it had, so she could understand why Silica and Leafa felt the fatigue bearing down on them.

But what was odd was the way the little dragon Pina—which should have been a simple collection of algorithms—would take off from Silica's shoulders and curl up on top of Kirito whenever he was sleeping nearby.

It almost made her wonder if Kirito was emitting some kind of "sleep parameter" as he was snoozing. As evidence of that, she'd just been wide awake and absorbed in her report, but now her body felt weightless…

"Hey, now *you're* sleeping, Asuna! And Liz, too!"

She bolted upright, feeling Silica shaking her shoulder. Across the table, Lisbeth snapped up, too, blinking furiously. The girl smiled shyly and shook her pink hair, which gleamed with the metallic shine characteristic of leprechauns.

"You can't help but get sleepy, watching him...I wonder one of those illusion magic things that spriggans do."

"Hee hee! I doubt it. I'll wake us up by putting on some tea. The instant kind, though."

Asuna stood up and pulled four cups out of the cupboard behind her. They were magical mugs that produced a random flavor of tea out of ninety-nine varieties with a single tap—a recent quest reward.

With the mugs and some fruit tarts on the table, the four girls, including the now-awake Silica, each took a sip of a different kind of hot liquid.

"By the way," Lisbeth started, as though remembering something, "have you heard about the Absolute Sword, Asuna?"

"The rumors started going around regularly just before the end of the year...so about a week ago," Lisbeth said, then nodded to herself in understanding. "Oh, right, no wonder you didn't know, then. You were in Kyoto at the end of December."

"Please don't remind me of that unpleasant stuff when I'm playing a game," Asuna said, frowning. Lisbeth laughed loudly.

"I guess it's hard being a rich girl from a rich family."

"It *was* hard! I had to spend all day in a full kimono and proper sitting position, greeting people. I couldn't even enjoy a quick dive at night, because the building I was staying in didn't even have wireless! I brought my AmuSphere with me, and it was all for nothing."

She sighed and drained the last of her tea.

At the end of January, Asuna was essentially forced into a trip to the Yuuki household headquarters—her paternal grandparents' home in Kyoto—with her parents and older brother. The rest of the family at large was very worried about her two-year "hospitalization." She couldn't very well refuse a trip to see them all and thank them for their concern and help during that time.

When she was younger, spending the start of the year back home was an ordinary event, and she enjoyed seeing all the cousins around her age. But somewhere around the time she got into middle school, Asuna found this tradition to be more and more suffocating.

The main Yuuki family was a line that had been in the currency exchange business in Kyoto for, without exaggeration, more than two centuries. They had lasted through the Meiji Restoration and the chaos of war, and they now ran a regional bank that had offices all throughout western Japan. Her father, Shouzou Yuuki, had grown RCT into a major electronics manufacturer in a single generation thanks to the ample funds provided by the main family business. The extended family was positively littered with company presidents and government officials.

Naturally, like Asuna and her brother, all of the cousins were "good students" at "good schools," sitting politely at the family table as their parents boasted about the award their child had won in a recent competition and the national rank their child scored recently on a standardized test. These conversations were pleasant on the surface, but that only hid the fierce current of rivalry running underneath. When Asuna began to recognize this atmosphere and feel alienated by it, the whole exercise struck her as nothing more than the family ranking its own children by value.

In November 2022, the winter of her last year of middle school, Asuna fell prey to *SAO* and wasn't rescued until January of 2025, exactly one year ago. That made this her first visit to the family gathering in four years. The main family house was a massive mansion in the Kyoto teahouse style. She was put into a tight, long-sleeved kimono and forced to greet countless relatives, starting with her grandparents, until she began to feel like an NPC whose only purpose was offering formal pleasantries.

Still, she enjoyed seeing her cousins again, but there was something in their eyes when they rejoiced at seeing her alive and well that she did not like.

They all pitied her. They showered her with sympathy: the first competitor to fall off the track in the race they'd all been in since the moment they were born. She wasn't just overthinking this; ever since she was a child, Asuna had known how to read what people were thinking from their demeanor.

Naturally, she was now a completely different person than she had been before. That world, and more important, that boy, had reborn her into someone else, whether she wanted it or not. So the pity of her cousins, aunts, and uncles passed through her mind without raising so much as a ripple. She was a swordsman above all else, someone who fought with her own strength—a belief that still remained firm within her heart, even after the passing of the world that taught her that.

But she knew that her cousins, who only saw VRMMOs as an evil influence, would never understand her philosophy. Neither would her mother, who was irritable during the entire stay in Kyoto.

There wasn't a shred left of Asuna's former belief that she had to get into a good college to land a good job. She liked her current school very much, and over the next year, she would spend her time finding what she truly wanted to do. Her ultimate goal in life, of course, was to start a family with a boy one year her junior, but in the real world this time.

Such was the thought Asuna kept in her mind as she grinned her way through her relatives' prying questions, but the one event that finally got to her occurred on the day before she returned to Tokyo, when she found herself isolated in a back room of the main mansion with a second cousin who was two years her elder.

He was the son of some kind of executive at the family's bank, and he went on and on endlessly about his major in college, the bank where he was already promised a job out of school, what his position would be, and how he would rise through the ranks. Asuna kept her smile plastered on her face to feign interest, but in the back of her mind, all she sensed was some kind of underhanded scheme on the part of the adults, in the way they had isolated the two of them like this...

"Are you listening, Asuna?"

She came back to her senses when Lisbeth poked Asuna's foot beneath the table.

"Oh! S-sorry. Just thinking about some unpleasant stuff."

"Oh yeah, what's that? Did they try to set you up with a husband in Kyoto?"

"..."

"...Why is your face twitching? Wait...are you saying I was—"

"No, you're wrong! It was nothing!" Asuna protested, shaking her head furiously. She tapped the lip of her empty mug and chugged down the oddly purple tea that appeared. Once done with that, she was ready to change the subject by any means necessary.

"So...this really tough player. Is it a PKer?"

"No, a PVPer—proper duels. You know how, north of the main city on the twenty-fourth floor, there's a little tourist island with a huge tree on it? Every day at three o'clock, the duelist shows up at the foot of the tree and duels challengers one by one."

"Oooh. Is it someone from a tournament?"

"Nope, totally new face. But the skill numbers must be off the charts, so maybe they converted from another game. At first, there were just posts on *MMO Tomorrow*'s forum looking for opponents. So about thirty people got together to show 'this *ALO* newb' a lesson about running your mouth...'"

"And they got whooped?"

"Every single one. Not a single person managed to score more than thirty percent damage, so it was legit overkill."

"I don't know if I can believe this."

Silica butted in, chewing on a fruit tart. "It took me almost half a year to learn how to handle air battle, and this person was just zipping around right after conversion!"

"Conversion" was the system for transferring characters between all the VRMMOs created from the Seed platform, which included *ALO*. A character could be taken from one game to another relatively easily, keeping a similar level of base stats. However, no money or items could be transferred. Naturally, the finer points of mastering a new game had to come from experience.

"Did you try, Silica?" Asuna asked. Silica shook her head, eyes wide.

"No way! I watched the duels, but I knew I couldn't win. Liz and Leafa tried, though. They're both the bold type, I suppose."

"Oh, shuddup," Liz quipped.

"It was a learning experience," said Leafa. Asuna smiled at the banter but was surprised on the inside. Lisbeth was one thing—she was playing a combat-weak race, and she prioritized her blacksmithing skills. But anyone who could defeat Leafa—probably the best air warrior of the sylphs—was a force to be reckoned with. And fresh after conversion? It was nearly unthinkable.

"Sounds like the real deal to me. I'm starting to get intrigued."

"Heh! I figured you'd say that, Asuna. The only ones in the monthly tournaments who haven't tried their hand yet are big shots like Lady Sakuya and General Eugene, and they aren't really in a position to engage in street duels."

"But if you keep overwhelming everybody, won't you just run out of opponents eventually? Unlike the tournaments, a street duel has really stiff experience penalties for dying, right?"

"You'd think so, but no—the draw is what's being wagered," Silica interjected again.

"Oh? Are they betting some kind of superrare item?"

"It's not an item. It's an Original Sword Skill. A supertough mega-attack."

Asuna just barely managed to keep herself from mimicking a classic Kirito move and ended up shrugging with a whistle of amazement instead.

"An OSS, huh? What kind? How many hits?"

"Um, from what I saw, it's an all-purpose, one-handed sword attack. The thing is, it's an eleven-hit combo."

"Eleven!"

This time, she couldn't help but purse her lips and let out a high-pitched whistle.

Sword Skills were the signature gameplay system of the old *Sword Art Online*. Each category of weapon had its own pre-programmed skills, from deadly single-blow attacks to furious combinations. What set them apart from ordinary weapon attacks was a particular initial motion that the game recognized, at which point it would automatically "assist" players by moving them through the entire attack at maximum speed. Each Sword Skill had unique visual and audio effects that distinguished it, and using them made the player feel like an invincible superwarrior.

As part of the massive update that added Aincrad to *ALO*, the game's new administrators undertook the bold decision to reinstate the Sword Skill system almost exactly as it had existed in *SAO*.

In essence, the very fundamental battle system of New *ALO* underwent a revolution. Naturally, it led to major debates among the player base, but once the dissenters had a chance to experience Sword Skills for themselves, they were all entranced.

Until that point, all the flashiest effects of *ALO* were the sole province of magic spells, and magic was also superior in accuracy and range, which left close-combat physical fighters in a small minority. The advent of Sword Skills helped even out that balance. Even more than half a year since the update, the combination of air battle and Sword Skills was producing heated commentary and debate among the game's community.

But the adventurous new developers were not content just to borrow the Sword Skill system they'd inherited from those who came before them.

They developed and implemented a new addition to the system called Original Sword Skills. As the name suggested, these were user-created skills. Unlike the preexisting skills that had specific motions and details already created by the devs, these were Sword Skills that players could create and register for themselves.

As soon as it was unlocked, countless players pulled out their weapons in town and wilderness, envisioning their own supercool finishing move—and were instantly plunged into deep despair and frustration.

The method to register an Original Sword Skill (OSS) was extremely simple.

Just open the menu, go to the OSS tab and, from there, into the "skill entry" mode. Hit the skill-recording button, swing your weapon to your heart's content, then hit the stop button when done. It was as simple as that.

However, for the user-created ultimate attack to be recognized by the game as a Sword Skill, it had to fulfill certain extremely stringent requirements. Nearly all variations of simple slashes and thrusts already existed in the game as Sword Skills. That meant that any OSS had to be a combination attack, by necessity. But there had to be absolutely no waste in the movement, trajectory, balance of weight, and so on, and on top of that, the action had to match the speed of the finished Sword Skill.

In other words, the player had to prove the nearly paradoxical: that he could replicate his combination at superhuman speed already, without any help from the system.

The only way to overcome this hurdle was a blinding amount of practice and repetition. The movements had to be burned into the synapses of the brain.

Almost everyone who tried it gave up on the dream of his or her own super–combo attack, unable to handle the endless slog of so much practice. But a few hardy souls managed to develop and register their own OSSs, earning them an honor much like the classic sword schools of the feudal era. Indeed, some of them went on to start guilds titled the "_____ School," effectively running their own in-game dojos.

It was the "skill inheritance" function of the OSS system that made it possible for such schools to exist. Anyone who successfully created an OSS could pass a first-generation copy to other players through an item called a Skill Tome.

An OSS was devastating against monsters as well as other players. Everyone wanted one. Soon the asking price for secondhand skills grew astronomical, with Skill Tomes of combinations of more than five hits ranking among the most expensive items in *ALO*'s economy. The strongest widely known OSS at present was General Eugene's eight-part "Volcanic Blazer," but he had no need for money and hadn't taught it to anyone yet.

For her own part, Asuna had successfully created a five-part OSS after months of practice, but the process had drained her so completely that she didn't feel like working on a new skill anytime soon.

So it was within this context that the mysterious "Absolute Sword" appeared, wielding an unprecedented eleven-hit skill.

"Well, that would explain why everyone wants a duel, then. Has everyone seen this Skill for themselves?" Asuna asked. All three of them shook their heads. Lisbeth spoke for the group.

"No, apparently it was displayed for all to see on the very first day of these street duels but hasn't been used since…I guess you could say that no one's been able to even pressure the Absolute Sword enough to elicit the use of the OSS."

"Not even Leafa?"

Leafa's shoulders slumped. "It was a close fight until both of us were at about sixty percent…and it took nothing more than default moves to finish me off the rest of the way."

"Wow…Oh, that reminds me, I'm missing some basic details. What race, what weapon are we talking about?"

"Oh, an imp. And the weapon was a one-handed sword, but one almost as thin as Asuna's rapier. Basically, they were superfast. Even the normal attacks were about as quick as a skill…You could barely follow it with the naked eye. I've never seen anything like it before."

"A speed type, huh? If even Leafa couldn't keep up with it, then I don't stand a chance…Oh!" Asuna suddenly remembered something important. "When it comes to speed, the most ridiculous person of all is sleeping right over there. What about Kirito? I bet he'd be interested in this."

Lisbeth, Silica, and Leafa all shared a look, then burst into laughter at once.

"Wh-what? What is it?" Asuna stammered.

To her shock, Leafa giggled. "Hee hee. Oh, Big Brother already tried. He was very cool in defeat, though."

"Def…?"

He lost. Kirito *lost*.

Asuna's mouth fell open and stayed there for several seconds.

To Asuna, Kirito as a swordsman had become a stand-in for the concept of "absolute power." In both *SAO* and *ALO*, as far as Asuna knew, the only person to ever beat Kirito in a one-on-one duel was Heathcliff, commander of the Knights of the Blood, and that was only due to his unfair advantage as the (secret) game administrator.

Though she'd never told Lisbeth and the others about it, Asuna herself had once crossed blades with Kirito in a deadly serious duel in *SAO*. It happened around the time that Asuna had assumed the lead of the KoB forces on the front line as the vice commander of the guild, just after she first met Kirito.

There was a face-off about the strategy to defeat a particular field boss, with the split happening between the KoB's speed-prioritizing faction and Kirito, who spoke for a number of other solo players. There was no compromise to be found between the two sides, so it ended with a virtual coin flip: a duel between the leader of each faction.

At the time, Asuna already had an interest in Kirito as a person, but the rest of her was trying to snuff out that desire. She believed that personal sentiment could not be allowed to override the duty of beating the game.

Asuna thought that a duel was the perfect opportunity to quash the weaker side of her heart. By defeating Kirito and efficiently dispatching the boss after that, she could regain her logical, bloodless side.

But she did not know about the hidden strength behind the otherwise lackluster-looking swordsman.

Their duel was a truly ferocious battle. With each collision of their blades, Asuna felt her troubles escaping from her mind, leaving only the delight of fighting against a worthy foe. For nearly ten minutes, they exchanged brain pulses on a level that she had never experienced before, but she didn't even register the passage of time.

Asuna lost that fight. She reacted to Kirito's desperate feint—he reached for the second, unequipped sword on his back, for reasons she learned later—and he made use of that opportunity to land a clean hit on her.

Against her rational desire, Asuna's romantic leanings became impossible to ignore after this duel, and in addition to that personal sentiment, Kirito's freewheeling sword style put another impression into her mind.

He was the strongest swordsman alive. Even now that the Black Swordsman of *SAO* was no more, that image remained as fresh and vivid as ever.

So the revelation that this "Absolute Sword" had beaten Kirito was so unthinkable, so shocking, that shivers ran across her skin.

Asuna looked from Leafa to Lisbeth and rasped, "Was Kirito… fighting his hardest?"

"Hmmm," Lisbeth mumbled, crossing her arms. "I hate to say it, but when you get to fighting at that level, I can't tell what's serious and what's not…I mean, Kirito wasn't using two swords, so in that sense, I guess he wasn't fighting at his best. Besides…"

She trailed off and looked over at the sleeping Kirito, ruby eyes glittering with the reflection of the fire. There was a faint smile curling the sides of her mouth.

"I get the feeling that in a normally functioning game, Kirito won't ever fight with all of his strength again. Meaning that, the only time he fights his hardest is when the game is no longer a game, and the virtual world becomes real…Which means it's for the best if he never feels he needs to fight his hardest again. He's already got a knack for getting involved in trouble."

"…"

Asuna stared at the sleeping black-haired warrior herself, then nodded. "Yeah...you're right."

Leafa and Silica bobbed their heads as well, each bearing expressions of their own understanding. Leafa, who was Kirito's sister in real life, eventually broke the silence.

"Well, as far as I could tell...he was taking it completely seriously. At the very least, he definitely was not going easy on his opponent. Plus..."

"...What?"

"I'm not entirely sure, but just before the duel finished, they were locked to the hilt for a moment, and I think I saw him speaking with the Absolute Sword about something...After that, they took their distance again, and he wasn't able to dodge away from the next charge attack..."

"Hmm...I wonder what they were talking about."

"Well, I asked, but he wouldn't tell me. I feel like there's something there, though."

"I see. In that case, he probably won't tell me, either." Asuna looked down at her hands and mumbled, "I guess the only way to find out is to ask this Absolute Sword directly."

Lisbeth raised her eyebrows. "You gonna fight?"

"Well, I doubt I'll win. It sounds like this Absolute Sword person came to *ALO* for a purpose. Something more than just challenging people to duels."

"Yeah, I get the same feeling. But I bet you won't learn the answer unless you put up as good a fight as Kirito did. Which character you gonna go as?"

Asuna thought over Lisbeth's question. In addition to her undine fencer Asuna, converted from her old *SAO* player data, she also had a sylph named Erika whom she'd started from scratch. She decided to try out a different character for the simple reason of wearing a different face now and then.

Erika's build was a dagger-based close-combat fighter, which made her better suited for duels than Asuna, who was half healer. But she shrugged immediately.

"I'll go with the one I'm more familiar with. If the opponent's a speed type, it'll be more about reaction time than pure DPS numbers. Will you guys be coming along?"

As she faced the group, all three of them nodded simultaneously. Silica's tail wagged happily through the space on the back of the chair as she piped up, "Of course! I wouldn't miss this fight for the world."

"I don't know how much of a fight it'll be...but that's settled, then. The little island on the twenty-fourth floor at three o'clock, you said? Let's meet up here at two thirty, then," Asuna suggested, clapping her hands and bringing up her menu to check the time.

"Oh crap, it's already six. I'm going to be late for dinner."

"Shall we call it a day, then?" Leafa asked, saving her homework progress and cleaning up. As the others followed her lead, the sylph snuck over to the rocking chair, grabbed the back, and violently shook it back and forth.

"Wake up, Big Brother! We're leaving!"

Asuna watched the scene with a grin, but a sudden thought wiped it away. She turned to Lisbeth.

"Hey, Liz."

"What?"

"You said the Absolute Sword might be a converted player," she began quietly. "With that much strength, it makes me wonder... could it be a former *SAO* player?"

Liz nodded seriously. "Yeah, I wondered that myself. After Kirito's fight, I asked him what he thought..."

"And what did he say?"

"He said there was no way that the Absolute Sword could have been an *SAO* player."

"..."

"Because if that were the case...it wouldn't have been him who won the Dual Blades skill."

2

Chi-chik.

A short electronic tone signaled the powering off of the AmuSphere.

Asuna opened her eyes slowly. She felt the chilly damp of the room's air before her eyes could focus on the ceiling of the dim room.

She'd set her air conditioner to provide a bit of warmth but forgot to disable the timer, so it had run its cycle and turned off while she was in the dive. The room, which was a bit too big for her, was now at thermal equilibrium with the outside temperature. She heard the sound of rain and turned to the large window at her right to see countless droplets clinging to the outside of the dark glass.

Asuna shivered and sat up in bed. She reached for the room environment controller embedded in the set of drawers at her side and tapped the "automatic" button on the touch panel. That was all it took for two curtain motors to quietly buzz to life and shut out the windows, the air conditioner to come awake, and the LED lights on the ceiling to emit an orangey glow.

Her room was outfitted with the latest interior systems offered by RCT's home division. They'd installed all of these things while she was hospitalized, but for some reason, Asuna couldn't bring herself to appreciate them. It was completely natural to control everything about an inside room with a single menu in VR, but something about that concept coming to the real world left her cold. She imagined she could feel on her skin the machine gaze of all the sensors embedded into the floor and walls.

Or perhaps she felt it was so cold because now she could compare it to the warmth of Kazuto Kirigaya's traditional home, which she'd visited several times. Her grandparents' house on her mother's side was like that one. When she went there during summer vacations, she'd sit facing the back garden, her legs dangling off the wooden porch in the sunlight, eating her grandma's shaved ice. Those grandparents had died years ago, and the house had since been torn down.

She sighed and stuck her feet into her slippers before getting up. The motion made her head swim, and she tilted over. There was no avoiding the powerful gravity of the real world.

The virtual world simulated the same level of gravity, of course. But the Asuna in that world could leap nimbly and allow her soul to wander freely through the air. The gravity of the real world wasn't just a physical force; it contained the weight of many different things that dragged her down to earth. She was tempted to fall back onto the bed, but it was nearly time for dinner. For every minute she was late, she'd get an extra rebuke from her mother.

She dragged her heavy feet to the closet, where the door folded itself open without any prompting on her part. She took off her loose polar fleece wear and threw it rebelliously on the floor. Once she had changed into a spotlessly white blouse and a long, dark cherry skirt, she sat down on the stool of the nearby dresser, which automatically deployed a three-sided mirror and a bright overhead light.

Even around the house, Asuna's mother did not suffer her to dress casually. She picked up a brush and tidied the long hair that had gone messy during her dive. As she did, she wondered what sort of scenes were playing out at that moment at the Kirigaya home over in Kawagoe.

Leafa (Suguha) had said that she and Kazuto were both on dinner duty tonight. Suguha would drag a sleepy-looking Kazuto downstairs. They'd stand in the kitchen, Suguha with the knife and Kazuto cooking a fish. Before long, their mother would return and enjoy an evening beer as she watched television. The meal would come together as they chatted back and forth, until steaming dishes and bowls were placed on the table, and the three said their grace.

Asuna let out a trembling breath and tried not to cry. She put down the brush and stood up. After taking a step into the dim hallway, the lights behind her went out before she could even close the door.

She descended the semicircular staircase to the first-floor hall, where the housekeeper, Akiyo Sada, was about to open the front door. She was probably on her way home after fixing dinner.

Asuna bowed to the woman, a petite figure in her early forties. "Good evening, Mrs. Sada. Thank you for coming again. Sorry to always keep you so late."

Akiyo shook her head, her eyes wide in consternation as she bowed deeply. "N-not at all, Mistress. It is my job."

The last year had taught her that saying, "Call me Asuna" would be pointless. Instead, she approached the housekeeper and quietly asked, "Are Mother and Brother home already?"

"Master Kouichirou will be home late. Madam is already in the dining room."

"...I see. Thank you; sorry to keep you."

Once again, Asuna bowed and Akiyo bent over deeply at the waist before pushing the heavy door open and scurrying out.

She knew the woman had a child in elementary or middle school. Their home was also in the ward of Setagaya, but she wouldn't get home after shopping until at least seven thirty. That was a long time for a growing child to wait for dinner. She'd tried suggesting to her mother that they could have precooked dinners, but the idea was never entertained.

Asuna spun on her heel, hearing three different locks click on the door behind her, and crossed the hall to the dining room. The instant she pushed open the heavy oaken door, a quiet but taut voice said, "You're late."

She glanced at the clock on the wall, which was at exactly six thirty. Before she could protest this fact, the voice continued. "Come to the table five minutes before the meal."

"...I'm sorry," Asuna grunted, stepping onto the thick rug with her slippers as she approached the table. She lowered herself into the high-backed chair, eyes downcast.

At the center of the three-hundred-square-foot dining room was a long, eight-legged table. Asuna's seat was the second from the northeast corner. To her left was her brother Kouichirou's chair, and on the short, adjacent east end was her father Shouzou's, but both were empty now.

In the chair across the table and to the left was her mother, Kyouko Yuuki, a glass of her favorite sherry in hand, glancing through an original edition of a book on economics.

She was quite tall for a woman. She was thin, but her solid structure kept her from looking fragile. Her shiny, dyed-brown hair was parted evenly on both sides and cropped straight across her shoulder line.

Though her features were attractive, the sharpness of the bridge of her nose, the line of her jaw, and the fine but deep wrinkles around her mouth gave her an undeniable air of severity. Then again, perhaps this effect was intended. Through her sharp tongue and political shrewdness, she had dispatched her department rivals and achieved tenure as a professor at just forty-nine years of age last year.

Kyouko shut the hardcover and did not look up as Asuna sat. She spread her napkin over her lap, picked up her knife and fork, and only then did she glance at her daughter's face.

For her part, Asuna looked down, mumbled a formality, then picked up her spoon. For a time, the only sound in the dining room was the faint clinking of silverware.

The meal was a greens salad with blue cheese, fava bean potage, grilled white fish with herb sauce, whole-wheat bread, and so on. Kyouko selected each day's meals for maximum nutrition, but naturally, she cooked none of it.

Asuna continued to eat, wondering when these lonely meals with her mother had become such tense, unpleasant affairs. Perhaps they had always been this way. She remembered being scolded sharply for spilling soup or leaving vegetables behind. It was just that in the past, Asuna had never known what a fun and pleasant meal was, by comparison.

As she mechanically ate her meal, Asuna's mind wandered far away through her memory to her virtual home, until Kyouko's voice brought her back. "Were you using that machine again?"

Asuna glanced at her mother and nodded. "Yes…We made an agreement to do our homework together."

"It's not going to sink in and do you any good unless you do that studying on your own."

Clearly, telling Kyouko that she *was* doing the work on her own in that virtual environment was not going to convince her. Asuna kept her face down and tried a different tack. "Everyone lives very far apart. In there, we can meet one another instantly."

"Using that machine does not count as 'meeting.' Besides, homework is meant to be done alone. With your friends, you're bound to end up cavorting around," Kyouko said, her speech picking up steam as she tilted back the sherry. "And you don't have the leeway for fun and games. You're behind the others, so it's obvious that you need to study even harder to make up those two extra years."

"…I am doing my studies. Didn't you see the printout of my second-term grade report I left on your desk?"

"I did, but I put no stock in the grade reports from a school like that."

"A school like…what?"

"Listen, Asuna. I'm giving you a home tutor in addition to

school for your third term. Not one of these popular online tutors, but a proper one who comes to the house."

"W-wait…This is so sudden…"

"Look at this," Kyouko commanded, cutting off Asuna and picking up a tablet computer off the table. Asuna took it from her and looked at the screen, frowning.

"…What is this…? A summary of a…transfer exam?"

"I called in a favor from a friend who's a high school director to allow you to take a transfer exam for their senior program. Not a slapped-together school like your current one, but a real school. It works on credits, so you could fulfill the graduation requirements in the first semester. That way, you can be in college starting in September."

Asuna stared at her mother's face in shock. She put down the tablet and raised her hand to keep Kyouko from continuing. "W-wait. You can't just decide that on your own. I like my school. The teachers there are nice, and it's a good, proper school. I don't need to transfer," she squeaked.

Kyouko sighed and made a show of closing her eyes, holding her temples with her fingers, and leaning back against the chair. This was her finely honed conversation technique to convince the other person of her superior position. No doubt any man who witnessed this trick on the sofa of the professor's office would shrink up. Even her husband, Shouzou, seemed to avoid offering any antagonistic opinions around the house.

"Your mother looked into this properly," Kyouko lectured. "The place you're attending now can hardly be called a school. Their curriculum is slapdash and the subjects are shallow. They scraped together anyone they could get for a faculty, hardly any of which have experience. It's less of an academic institution than a correctional facility."

"You…you can't say that…"

"It all sounds very nice when you call it a school that accepts students whose education has fallen behind due to an accident. But in reality, it's nothing more than a place where they can gather potential future problem children to keep an eye on them. Perhaps there's a function for such a place, when some of those children have spent all that time killing one another in some bizarre game, but there's no reason for *you* to be there."

"..."

It was such an avalanche of withering criticism that Asuna could not speak.

The school campus situated in western Tokyo that she'd been attending since last spring was indeed a hastily built school, constructed just two months after it was announced. The purpose of it was to educate those players who had been trapped in the deadly *Sword Art Online* and lost two years of their education. Any former *SAO* player under the age of eighteen could attend without an entrance test or any tuition, and a graduate automatically earned the right to sit for a college entrance exam— treatment that was so favorable, some people even complained about it.

But Asuna knew from her attendance at the school that it was more than just a safety net. All students were required to undergo individual counseling once a week, where they were subjected to questions meant to detect antisocial behavior or thoughts. Depending on the answers, they could be reinstitutionalized or given drugs to take. So Kyouko's accusation that it was a "correctional facility" was not entirely untrue.

Even if that was the case, Asuna loved her "school." No matter the government ministries' intentions, the teachers who worked there were all volunteers who earnestly sought to connect with the students. There was no need to hide her past from the other kids, and she got to spend time with the friends she'd made: Lisbeth, Silica, a number of the frontline warriors—and Kirito.

She bit her lip, still clutching the fork, and struggled with a sudden urge to reveal all of her most fervent inner feelings to her mother.

I'm exactly one of those children who spent all that time killing others. I was living in a world where lives were taken and lost by the sword every day. And I don't regret those days even the tiniest bit...

But Kyouko did not seem to detect her daughter's inner conflict. "You're not going to advance into a good college coming out of a school like that. You're already eighteen, don't you see? And at this rate, I can't begin to imagine when you'll be in college, if you stick with that place. Every one of your friends from middle school is about to take the standardized college exam next week. Don't you feel pressured to catch up?"

"There shouldn't be a serious problem if I'm a year or two late to get into college. Besides, going to college isn't the only kind of career path to go down..."

"That's preposterous," Kyouko rebuked sternly. "You have talent. You know what incredible pains your father and I have gone through to bring out that talent to the fullest. And then you lost two years to that crazy game...I wouldn't be saying this to you if you were an ordinary child. But you're not ordinary, are you? It would be a sin to let the talent you have go untapped. You have the ability to go to a great college and receive a first-class education—and that's what you ought to do. You can take your talents to the government or a business, or you can stay in school and make a living in academia. I'm not going to interfere with your choice. The one thing I will not allow you to do, however, is completely *abandon* those opportunities."

"There's no such thing as hereditary talent," Asuna managed to squeeze in when Kyouko stopped her speech for a breath. "You have to seize your own life, don't you? When I was younger, I thought that getting into a good college and finding a good job was all there was to life. But I changed. I don't have an answer yet, but I think I'm close to finding out what I really want to do. I want to attend this school for one more year so I can find it."

"Why would you limit your own options? You could spend years at that place and never create any kind of opportunity for yourself. But this transfer location is different. The college it feeds into is excellent, and if your marks are good, you can even get into my graduate school. Listen to me, Asuna—I just don't want you to make your life miserable. I want you to have a career that you can be proud of."

"My career...? Then what was up with that man you forced me to meet at the house over New Year's? I don't know what sort of story you fed him...but he seemed to think that we were already engaged. The only one who's limiting my life options is you, Mother."

Asuna couldn't keep her voice from trembling a bit. She was trying to keep her gaze as level and powerful as possible, but Kyouko only put the sherry to her lips, completely unperturbed.

"Marriage is a part of a career. Put yourself into a marriage that limits your material freedom, and you'll regret it in five or ten years. You won't be able to do those things you say you want to do. You won't have any trouble with Yuuya in that regard. And there's much more stability in a family-run regional bank than a megabank with all the internal competition that it involves. I happen to like Yuuya. He's a good, honest boy."

"...You haven't learned a thing, have you? Don't forget that the one who started that terrible crime spree, hurt me and many others, and nearly destroyed RCT was your personal choice for me: Nobuyuki Sugou."

"Don't even start," Kyouko said, grimacing and waving at the air as though swatting an invisible fly. "I don't want to hear about him. Besides...it was your father who was so enamored with that man that he wanted him for a son-in-law. He's never been a good judge of character. Don't worry about Yuuya; he might not be as ambitious or forceful, but that just makes him safer and more stable."

It was true that Shouzou, her father, had a bad habit of ignoring those who were closest to him. He focused on running the business first and foremost; even after leaving the CEO position, he was too busy tweaking deals with foreign capital sources to come home anymore. He admitted that it was a weakness of his that he'd been too obsessed with Sugou's development skills and vast ambitions and didn't pay any attention to the toxic human personality behind the business acumen.

But Asuna felt that one of the reasons for Nobuyuki Sugou's increasingly aggressive behavior since her middle school years was the incredible pressure that was placed upon him. And part of that pressure was undoubtedly the attitude that Kyouko exhibited.

Asuna swallowed a bitter lump in her throat and kept her voice hard. "At any rate, I have zero intention of getting along with him. I'll choose my own partner."

"Fine, as long as it's a good man who suits you. And let me be clear: That does not include any of the students at that facility."

"…"

Something about the way Kyouko said that made it seem oddly specific, and Asuna felt another chill run through her.

"Did you…look into him…?" she rasped in shock. Kyouko did not confirm or deny the accusation; instead, she changed the subject.

"You have to understand, your father and I just want you to be happy. From the moment we picked out your kindergarten, that's been our only concern. I know that deep down, you regret getting involved on a whim with that game Kouichirou bought. So you tripped and lost your footing a little bit, but you can still recover. Only if you truly work for it, though. You can still have the most brilliant career, if you just put in the effort."

The best career for you, not me, Asuna thought bitterly.

Asuna and Kouichirou were only elements of Kyouko's personal "brilliant career." Kouichirou went to a first-rate college and was working his way up the ladder at RCT, to Kyouko's satisfaction. Asuna was meant to follow in his footsteps, but between the freakish *SAO* Incident and the damage to RCT's image caused by Sugou's malfeasance, Kyouko was clearly feeling that her own career was damaged.

Asuna didn't have the spirit to continue arguing. She put her fork and knife down next to her half-eaten meal and stood up. "Let me think about the transfer," she said.

But Kyouko's response was dry and clinical. "You have until next week to decide. Fill out the necessary fields by then, print out three copies, and leave them on my desk."

Asuna hung her head and turned for the door. She considered just going back to her room, but there was something in her chest she needed to expel. A step out into the hallway, she turned back and coldly called out, "Mother."

"...What?"

"You're ashamed of Grandma and Grandpa, aren't you? You're unhappy that you were born from a simple farming family, rather than some famous house with proper heritage."

Kyouko looked stunned for a moment, but the harsh furrows returned to her brows and lips immediately. "Asuna! Come over here!" she snapped.

Asuna was already closing the heavy teak door. She darted across the hall and raced up the stairs, yanking open her bed-room door.

The sensors immediately caught sight of her and automatically turned on the lights and heat. She walked over to the control panel on the wall, unbearably irritated, and shut down the environment control system. She then threw herself onto the bed and buried her face in her pillow, not caring if her expensive blouse got wrinkled.

She didn't mean to cry. As a swordsman, she swore never to cry tears of sadness or frustration again. But that oath only amplified the agony that strangled her lungs.

Somewhere inside her head, a voice mocked, *You think you're a swordsman? Just because you weren't half bad at swinging around a little digital sword in a stupid game? What good is that going to do you in the real world?* Asuna clenched her jaw.

She should have changed after meeting him in that other world. She should have quit blindly following someone else's values and learned to fight for what she ought to do.

But from the outside, what was actually different about her now, compared to before she'd been trapped there? She put on

a false smile like a little doll for the sake of her relatives, and she couldn't firmly refuse the life her parents had set up for her. If she could be what she believed was her true self only in the virtual world, then what was the point of coming back to reality at all?

"Kirito…Kirito." The name whispered through her trembling lips.

Kirito—Kazuto Kirigaya—still seemed to possess the hardy will he'd gained from *SAO* even now, more than a year after their return to the real world. He had to be dealing with his own pressures, but he never let it show on his face.

When she had asked him what his future goals were, he smiled shyly and said that he wanted to be on the side of the developer, rather than the player. And not for software like VRMMOs, but a new man–machine interface, a much closer and more intimate connection than the current full-dive technology, with its many limitations and regulations. Even now, he was active in tech forums both domestic and foreign, studying and exchanging opinions with others eager to advance the interface.

Asuna believed that he would continue to head straight for his goal without hesitation. If possible, she wanted to be with him all the way, following that same dream. She was hoping to go to school with him for the next year so that she could determine what she needed to study to make that happen.

But that possibility was now on the rocks, and Asuna was filled with the helpless feeling that she could not resist the forces compelling her.

"Kirito…"

She wanted to see him. It didn't have to be in the real world; she just wanted to go back to their little cabin so she could cry into his chest and reveal all of her troubles.

But she couldn't. The one whom Kirito loved wasn't this powerless Asuna Yuuki, but Asuna the Flash, mightiest fencer in all the land. That knowledge was like a heavy chain around her neck.

"You're strong, Asuna. Much stronger than me…"

Kirito's long-past words echoed in her ears. Maybe he would

distance himself from her, as soon as she revealed her weakness to him.

The thought terrified her.

Asuna stayed facedown on the bed until she eventually fell into a light sleep.

She saw herself walking arm-in-arm with Kirito through the shade of the trees, silver scabbard at her waist. But her other self was locked in a dark place, forced to watch silently as the pair laughed and chatted away.

In the midst of her bittersweet dream, Asuna pined to return to that world.

3

The twenty-fourth floor of Aincrad was a majority-water level, covered in lakes and swamps. The visual motif was very similar to the sixty-first floor, home of Asuna's past residence in Selmburg, though that wouldn't be open to the players of *ALO* for quite a while yet.

The name of the main town was Panareze, which was a man-made island placed in the center of a massive lake, with floating bridges in all directions connected to countless little islands.

Asuna observed the festival air of Panareze from across the water, her head resting against Kirito's shoulder. They were sitting side by side on the southern shore of a little island just north of the city. Behind them were green, leafy trees, while little waves lapped at their feet. The winds crossing the lake, warm for winter, rustled the fine grass around them.

"Hey, do you remember the first time you came to my place in Selmburg?" Asuna asked, looking up at Kirito.

He smiled and replied, "I don't mean to brag, but I'm really good at not remembering things..."

"Aww!"

"...But I do remember that one vividly."

"...Really?"

"Of course. Remember, I had just gotten that ultrarare food item, and you cooked it into a stew for me. Oh, man…that meat was delicious…I still think about it sometimes."

"Great! So all you remember is the food!" Asuna pouted, but her tone was jovial as she jabbed him in the chest. "Fine…I'll admit, I remember that part, too."

"Sheesh, don't take it out on me, then…Hey, do you think it's possible to recreate that stew in real life?"

"Hmm…It was similar to poultry, so I bet you could tweak the sauce just right…But actually, I'd prefer to keep that a memory. Isn't the thought of a dish you can never taste again kind of romantic?"

"Um, well, I suppose." Kirito nodded regretfully. Asuna couldn't help but laugh again. He smiled for her, then seemed to remember something. "Oh, right. Hey…"

"What?"

"We seem to be building up a good stockpile of yrd again, so… when they update and unlock the sixties, d'you want to get a place in Selmburg again? Like your old apartment?"

"Hmm." Asuna considered Kirito's proposal, but eventually she shook her head. "No, I'm fine. It wasn't as if everything was sunshine and rainbows when I was living there. We should use that money to help Agil open his store in Algade instead."

"*Great*, the return of the business that can squeeze blood from a stone. If I invest in him, I'm charging an arm and a leg in interest…"

"Wow, you're terrible."

They could have talked about the old Aincrad all day. As they chatted and laughed, Asuna noticed that the number of players flying from Panareze over toward their island was growing considerably. They all flew overhead, toward the large tree at the center of the isle.

"Well, I think it's about time. I gotta go," Asuna said, already regretting the loss of his body warmth. Kirito put on a serious expression.

"Asuna. If you're going to fight the Absolute Sword..."

"...Yeah?"

"Well...um, I guess, just...It'll be tough. Seriously."

She found his lack of conviction curious. "I've already heard all the stories from Liz and Leafa. And most important, even you couldn't win. I'm not assuming I'll stand a chance. I just want to see it for myself...In fact, I still can't envision you losing in a fight."

"There are plenty of folks out there tougher than me by now. It's just...this Absolute Sword is on a different level."

"Speaking of which, Leafa mentioned that you had a little conversation in the middle of your duel. What did you talk about?"

"Oh, ummm, just something I was wondering about..."

"Such as?"

"Er, well..."

She was acutely aware that there was something anxious in Kirito's gaze, and she blinked repeatedly, even more confused.

No matter how strong this Absolute Sword was, this wasn't the world of *SAO* any longer. Even if you failed to resign in time in a duel and ran out of HP, someone could just cast a resurrection spell to bring you back on the spot. You'd lose a bit of experience to the death penalty, but nothing a few hours of grinding couldn't restore.

But his answer was not what she expected.

"Basically, I said, 'You're a complete and total resident of this world, aren't you?' And the answer I got was a smile and an unbelievably quick thrust. It was...faster than should be possible..."

"A total resident of this world...? Meaning, like, someone without a real life?" Asuna asked curiously, but Kirito shook his head.

"No. I wasn't speaking about a single VRMMO world, but the Seed Nexus as a whole...Actually, not that, either. I guess I was implying more like...a child of the full-dive environment itself."

"What does...that mean...?"

"I don't want to give you any preconceptions. You should go and experience it for yourself."

He bopped her on the head. She blinked and heard the sound of several fairies descending on the other side of the tree behind them, followed by a familiar bellow.

"I swear, take my eyes off of you for a minute, and this is what happens!"

Asuna hastily got up and turned toward the sound of footsteps striding through the grass. Lisbeth appeared around the side of the tree trunk, her hands planted on her waist, framing her heavy apron. She glared down at Asuna.

"Sorry to interrupt, but it's time."

"I-I know that," stammered Asuna. She used her wings to get to her feet, and then checked that her equipment was right. She had a tunic of woven mithril and a matching skirt, boots, and gloves made of water-dragon hide, and a rapier with a hilt of crystal in the scabbard at her waist. Each piece had the best possible stats for items of its type. If she lost the duel, it wouldn't be because of her gear.

Once she had inspected all of her equipment and magical accessories, Asuna glanced at the clock in the lower right corner of her view. It was just past 2:50 in real time.

With a glance at Kirito next to her, followed by Lisbeth, Silica, Leafa, and Yui overhead, Asuna was ready.

"Okay, let's go!"

They flew in a low, flat line, heading for the center of the nameless island. Once the rows of leaves and branches cleared up, a large hill came into view. Overhead loomed the tremendous foliage of what looked like a miniature version of Yggdrasil, the World Tree. At the base of the tree was a gathering of numerous players, arranged in a large circle. A wave of cheers reached her ears; the duels had already begun.

The group found an empty spot within the circle, and no sooner had they landed than a single player fell screaming out of the sky. He landed at the foot of the tree roots headfirst with a great crash, sending a cloud of dust flying.

The salamander swordsman lay splayed out on the ground for a time before he finally sat up. He shook his head, clearing the cobwebs of the impact, and raised his hands high.

"I give! I surrender! I resign!"

The end-of-duel fanfare played overhead, followed by a louder round of applause. Around the crowd, people marveled at the sixty-seventh consecutive victory of the champion and the unlikelihood that *anyone* would end that streak. Asuna leaned back and gazed upward, trying to catch a glimpse of the winner.

Amid the dapple of the great branches, she spotted a silhouette descending in a curling spiral. It was smaller than she expected. From the reports, she expected a huge, brawny man, but if anything, the torso looked delicate, fragile. As the figure approached, the details became more and more apparent.

Creamy skin with touches of purple in the shade, the signature look of the imps. Long, straight hair a lustrous purplish-black. An obsidian breastplate that was softly rounded and a bluish-purple tunic with a long skirt flapping in the wind. A scabbard at the waist, long and black.

As Asuna watched in stunned surprise, the unbeaten Absolute Sword did a lithe spin before touching down delicately on tiptoe, transitioning to a theatrical bow with skirt held in fingertips and right hand pressed to the chest. An extra-loud round of cheers and whistles erupted from all around—particularly from the men in the audience.

The Absolute Sword popped back to a standing position with a dazzling smile and a cheeky little V-for-victory sign. The duelist was clearly shorter than Asuna, with a compact face; dimpled cheeks; a slightly upturned nose; and big, shining eyes as purple as amethyst.

Shock still coursing through Asuna's veins, she leaned over and elbowed Lisbeth in the side.

"...Excuse me, Liz."

"What?"

"The Absolute Sword is...a girl!"

"What, didn't I say that?"

"No, you didn't! Oh…in fact…"

Now she turned to glance sidelong at Kirito.

"The reason you lost isn't because…"

"N-no!" he protested, straight-faced, shaking his head adamantly. "I didn't go easy on her just because she's a girl. I was superserious about it. Really. At least…from partway on."

"Oh, I'm sure," she huffed, turning away.

Meanwhile, the salamander was at last up on his feet, shaking hands with the Absolute Sword with a smile, despite his defeat. He returned to the crowd, scratching his head in embarrassment. The black-haired girl with the crimson headband cast a low-level heal spell on herself and surveyed the crowd.

"So, um, who's up next?"

Her voice was just as high-pitched and bubbly as her avatar. There was an innocent playfulness to it that you wouldn't expect from a veteran fighter.

ALO was a game that did not allow for players to switch gender, so the player herself had to be female, but it did not take age and figure into account; the player's avatar was generated randomly. Still, there was a naturalness to her mannerisms and voice that made you want to believe they reflected her true age.

In the crowd around Asuna, she could hear people teasing one another and sounding reluctant to step forward—there was no rush to be the next opponent. It was Lisbeth's turn to elbow Asuna in the ribs.

"Well, go on."

"W-wait…I need to get my mind back in gear…"

"Oh, you'll get that in no time once you fight her. Now get going!"

"Ack!"

Asuna stumbled forward several steps with the force of Lisbeth's push. She avoided falling by spreading her wings, and when she looked up, she was staring right into the face of the girl nicknamed the Absolute Sword.

"Oh, do you want to fight, Miss?" she asked, grinning.

Asuna had no choice but to answer, "Er...sure, I guess," in a tiny squeak. Normally she would have engaged in some verbal sparring with her opponent before the match, but she was thrown off guard by not finding the large, imposing man she expected.

A bracing cheer rose from the crowd. Many of the people present recognized Asuna from her frequent appearances on the medal stand after the monthly dueling tournaments, and she heard her name repeated several times.

"Okay!" the girl chirped, snapping her fingers and motioning Asuna over.

With a deep breath, she summoned up her courage and stepped into the middle of the crowd. Once the crowd noise had died down, she asked, "So, are there any rules to the duel?"

"Of course. You can use all the magic and items you want. I'll only be using this," she announced, tomboyish, patting the hilt of her sword. With that innocent show of confidence, Asuna finally felt her sense of competition prickling.

...After a comment like that, I'd be a coward to use long-distance interference magic. You want a proper swordfight? I'll give you one. Asuna stroked the handle of her rapier.

At that moment, the girl called out confidently and loudly, "Oh, right. Do you prefer fighting on land or in the air?"

Asuna was taken aback—she had assumed they would be fighting in the air. She stopped herself in the act of drawing her blade.

"...You're fine with either one?"

The Absolute Sword nodded with a grin. Asuna suspected another bit of mental gamesmanship was at play, but there wasn't a hint of malice in the imp girl's smile. She simply believed that she would win in either arena, that was all.

If that was the case, Asuna would indulge her. "On the ground, then."

"Okay. Jumps are allowed, but no using your wings!" the girl bubbled, folding her distinctive wings behind her back. The batlike appendages quickly faded in color until they were nearly invisible. At the same time, Asuna held her shoulder blades as close as she could for two seconds, the action command to eliminate her wings. She heard a faint jingle over her shoulder, the sign that they were gone.

From the very first day that she dove into *ALO* as a proper player and not a prisoner, Asuna had mastered the "voluntary flight" system, which didn't have a handy flight stick. At this point she was able to hold her own in air battles against *ALO* vets who had been around since before Aincrad was added to the game.

But it was hard to get over the battle instincts that had seeped into her core over two long years in *SAO*. Fighting on land would actually be quite an advantage for her. She could feel the solidity of the ground from her toes to her heels.

Next, Asuna checked the color cursor of the girl who went by "Absolute Sword" by focusing her gaze in the vicinity of the girl long enough to automatically bring up a long, horizontal window. In addition to revealing the target's name, HP/MP bars, and any buff/debuff icons, the window's color identified the nature of their relationship to the viewer. The reason it was called a "color cursor" was because it shifted in tone depending on if the target was a friendly, neutral, or hostile race, or if it was a friend, guild-mate, or party member.

As it was their first meeting, Asuna couldn't yet see the girl's name—the space above the HP bar was blank. Instead, there was a small icon to the left of that known as a "guild tag," the sign that she was a member of a guild. This logo was player-customizable, and hers was a cute image of a pink heart with white wings. Asuna did not have a tag of her own, as she wasn't a member of a guild yet. The idea had arisen among her friends to start a guild on several occasions, but they'd never gone through with it.

The girl's brilliant red-purple irises fixed on Asuna's after a brief period of being off focus; she must have been checking Asuna's cursor in turn. She grinned and waved her right hand, bringing up a system window. Immediately following that, a window notifying her of an incoming duel offer burst into life with bold fanfare. At the top, it said:

YUUKI IS CHALLENGING YOU TO A DUEL.

So the girl's name was Yuuki—it was spelled with katakana, but the first thing that came to Asuna's mind was "courage." It was a fitting name for her—both cute and gallant at the same time.

At the bottom of the window were three options that she recognized from *SAO*: "first-strike mode," then "half-finish mode," and finally, "full-finish mode." In the old Aincrad, nearly every duel was first-strike, in which the first clean hit by either player ended the fight. A full-finish duel meant that the loser would die, and in half-finish mode, if the finishing blow was a critical hit, it could easily drop the loser's HP into extremely perilous territory.

Naturally, without the threat of death hanging over their heads, full-finish mode was selected. Asuna hit the OKAY button, thinking about how the times had changed. The name *Yuuki* appeared in the girl's cursor. That meant that from her end, she could see the name *Asuna* as well.

The duel window disappeared, replaced with a ten-second countdown. Asuna the Flash and Yuuki the Absolute Sword grabbed their hilts at the same time, drawing their blades forth. Two high-pitched *shinng*s overlapped.

Asuna's foe used a narrow, one-handed longsword, as dark and translucent as her obsidian armor. Based on its brilliance and detail, it looked to be the same rank of weapon as Asuna's. In other words, it probably didn't have an ultrarare, unknown Legendary trait.

Yuuki held her longsword at midheight and easily took a sideways stance. Meanwhile, Asuna kept her right hand close to her body with the rapier held horizontally. The cheering of the crowd faded away like the drawing of a wave.

She took a deep breath, then let it out. The countdown hit zero.

At the very moment that the word DUEL flashed between them,

Asuna leaped forward as far as she could. She closed the twenty feet between them in a blink, twisting her frame to the right.

"*Shi!*"

Her right hand shot forward like an arrow from a bow. With all of that inertia and torque behind her, she thrust twice just left of Yuuki's body center, then a moment later, once more to the right. They were ordinary attacks, not Sword Skills, so they weren't very fast, but they were unerringly precise. While she might be able to dodge the first two hits to the right, it would be impossible to dodge the last one.

Just as Asuna expected, Yuuki spun to the right to evade the initial jabs. But the third strike would sink right into the spot where she stopped...

Instead, Yuuki's own sword turned into a blur just before the rapier point hit her breastplate. The aim of Asuna's thrust was thrown off by just a bit, and a tiny spark shot up from the right side of her weapon.

By the time she realized her opponent had accurately parried the blindingly fast thrust, Asuna's sword had already just grazed the Absolute Sword's armor and flown past it.

The nape of Asuna's neck crawled with the anticipation of a counterattack. But if she pulled her sword back now, it would immobilize her body and make it an easier target. Rather than fight the momentum of her thrust, she spun left into it.

At the same time, she caught sight of a black sparkle leaping up toward the base of her neck.

"——!!"

The lightning flash of its speed sent a sharp thrill racing through Asuna's body. Her breath stopped, and she put so much force into her toe spin that her foot drilled into the ground.

There was short, fine grass at her feet, and the friction of that surface was set slightly lower than cobblestones or bare earth. That differential cost Asuna, and her right foot slipped, causing her whole body to buckle.

But that was fortunate, as it meant Yuuki's blade only grazed

Asuna's chest. A terrific shock wave roared right into her ear as it passed. If the game had ruled that it struck her hair, she would have lost about half of her light blue coif. Out of the corner of her eye, she saw the air waver with the expulsion of all that unleashed energy.

With her boots properly gripping the ground again, Asuna leaped hard to the right. She bounded again with her left foot so that she was a safe distance away.

Yuuki was unbalanced with the force of her attack, but she kept her smile in place as she retook her mid-level stance. Asuna tried to calm her racing heart enough to return that smile—but on the inside, there was a waterfall of cold sweat coursing through her.

An incoming thrust was nothing more than an approaching point, and the only way to avoid it was to step sideways out of its path, but the Absolute Sword had successfully deflected it by striking the side of Asuna's rapier.

It was less the speed of the counter than the incredible reflexes that stunned Asuna. Despite all of the stories of her might, the cute exterior of her opponent caused her to let her guard down, and now it was as if a cold bucket of water had been thrown onto her. She'd suspected that Kirito's defeat was due to the fact that he went easy on a girl, but now she realized that suspicion was unfair and untrue. Even he had never succeeded in parrying one of Asuna's best thrusts that easily.

She took a deep breath to steady herself. This was a formidable foe, but she wasn't much of a warrior if she was ready to give up after trading a single round of blows…

Suddenly, she heard a little voice in her ears.

Oh, now you're a warrior? In a stupid little game…

She gritted her teeth and shook the mental noise out of her head. This was another real world, and every battle here was deadly serious. It had to be that way.

Asuna swung her sword to hold it above her right shoulder, snapping herself into focus. This time she pointed it directly at her opponent.

If normal attacks weren't going to work, she'd have to risk using a Sword Skill. The problem was that every Sword Skill was followed by an unavoidable period of delay, so missing with any of her hits would leave her open to a fatal counterattack at the end. She needed to unbalance her foe somehow, to ensure that her skill would strike true. Asuna clenched her empty left hand.

When she leaped forward again, her mind was cold and focused. She could feel a sense of acceleration throughout her body, the burning of her nerves and synapses—a sensation she hadn't felt when fighting in the world of *ALO* yet.

This time, Yuuki came toward her as well. The smile was gone from her lips, but the crystal-purple eyes still sparkled.

Asuna swiped to the right to deflect an obsidian slash that came roaring down on her from above. In addition to the sparks and clanging, a tremendous shock ran through her hand. The girl leaped back, but Yuuki snapped her weapon forward instantly, as if it had no weight of its own. Swing after swing, so fast that reacting once seeing them would be too late. Asuna had to watch every detail of her opponent's moves to predict the next attack and then deflect or evade it. At times, one of their swords would land briefly, and both fighters' HP started to drop, but neither had secured a clean hit yet.

In the midst of this ultraspeed battle, Asuna was struck by a sudden *off* sensation.

Indeed, Yuuki's attack and reaction speed were frightfully quick. She might be faster than Kirito when it came to pure speed. But the only reasons Asuna could keep up were the enormous backlog of experience she had with battle in *SAO* and the straightforward nature of her opponent's attacks. There were no stop-and-start jolts or feints to throw off Asuna's sense of timing.

Maybe she just didn't have much experience fighting against human players, Asuna thought. If that was the case, just a single instant of surprise might be the key to victory.

Asuna evaded a three-part attack from upper right, upper left, and side left, then leaped forward at right, into Yuuki's wheelhouse.

They were practically touching. At this range, a single step wouldn't provide enough distance for either of them to dodge.

Asuna dropped down and prepared to thrust straight for the center of her opponent's body. Yuuki reacted and started to swipe upward from below.

At that instant, Asuna drew her right hand back and threw a quick left punch into her foe's unguarded body—she'd learned the Martial Arts skill from a training hall in the far-off capital of the gnomes. There was little damage, as she was not equipped with a knuckle-style weapon, but it carried a stun effect that wouldn't be present without the skill.

A dull thud ran through her fist, and Yuuki's eyes went wide with shock.

This would be her only chance. Asuna instantly initiated the four-part Quadruple Pain Sword Skill.

Her rapier flashed bright red, and her right, guided by the unseen hand of the game engine, ripped through the air like lightning.

Asuna was certain that her skill would land. Her opponent was off balance. She was at close distance. Evasion was impossible.

But as she let the system do all the work, Asuna was watching her opponent's face, and another shock ran down her back. The Absolute Sword's eyes were still wide, but there was no surprise in the reddish-purple irises. Her pupils were focused intently on the tip of the rapier.

She can follow the path of the sword?! Asuna marveled, just as Absolute Sword's right hand twitched.

Four quick, hard scrapes rang out, like the sound of a sword briefly being placed against a spinning whetstone. Asuna's four-part skill was deflected in all directions, without a single hit landing. All she'd seen was the black inkblot afterimage of Yuuki's sword.

After her final blow, Asuna was left frozen for less than a second with her hand outstretched—but the pause filled her with despair. The deadly Absolute Sword would not possibly pass on that opportunity.

The obsidian sword whipped backward and glowed bluish-purple.

A counter Sword Skill!

"Yaah!"

It was the first vocal utterance Yuuki had made in the duel. A direct thrust so fast that she couldn't have dodged it even without the skill delay bit into Asuna's left shoulder. It was followed by a breathless five-part combo. Every blow rang true, and Asuna's HP dropped quickly into the yellow. She didn't recognize this as a One-Handed Sword Skill, which meant it must be an Original Sword Skill. It was a tremendous five-part thrusting combo...

But throughout Asuna's absent admiration, Yuuki's sword never lost its brilliant shine. And now, she held it up to the left.

Five wasn't the end of the combo—there was more. A third shock ran through Asuna as she finally recovered after her skill delay.

Five more of the same thrusts meant she would run out of HP. But there was no way for her to dodge. If a futile attempt to escape got her cut across the back, she'd be better off putting all her hopes on a last-ditch attack. Asuna clenched her rapier and started another Sword Skill. It was the five-part OSS she'd managed to create, called "Starry Tear."

Bursts of red and blue intersected. In the same formation as the last five-part combo, Yuuki hit Asuna with an *X*-shaped attack starting at her right shoulder and crossing her body.

But this time, Asuna's rapier found purchase as well. Five thrusts bit into the black armor in a tiny star shape.

After they had traded five-hit skills, a moment of silence descended. Neither had fallen yet. Yuuki's HP bar was halfway drained and colored yellow. Asuna's HP was down in the red zone, just a tiny sliver left. As a character inherited from her old *SAO* data, Asuna's HP value was higher than even the oldest-running *ALO* member. And that stunning ten-part OSS had nearly finished her off entirely...

But no. Yuuki's longsword was *still* glowing purple. The Sword Skill wasn't over.

It drew back and aimed right for the center of the glowing *X* of damage that crossed Asuna's chest.

Eleven hits.

To her astonishment, she recognized that this was the very OSS that the Absolute Sword was wagering in the duel.

The power and speed were off the charts. And beyond that, it was beautiful. She had no regrets in being defeated by such a skill. Asuna closed her eyes and waited for the finishing blow.

The eleventh attack, which was poised to eradicate the last tiny line of health left on her HP bar, stopped still.

With the skill canceled, the tremendous light and impact of that blow scattered into empty air instead, rustling all the surrounding grass outward.

"——?!"

As Asuna stared wide-eyed, the Absolute Sword lowered her namesake and walked closer, of all things. She patted Asuna's shoulder with a free hand and gave her a dazzling grin. Her lips opened wide, and she made a bold proclamation.

"Yes, you're very good! I've decided on you!!"

"Wha…Err…?" Asuna stammered stupidly, taken aback. "Um… what about the duel…?"

"That was enough to satisfy me. Or did you want to keep going to the finish?" Yuuki replied with a smile. Asuna shook her head. Either way, her HP would have gone down to zero if she hadn't blocked the final attack.

The tomboy nodded happily, continuing. "I've been looking for someone who struck me as just right. I finally found you! So, do you have some free time still?"

"Uh…yes. I'm free…"

"Then come with me for a bit!"

Yuuki the Absolute Sword slid her blade coolly into the sheath on her waist and forcefully extended a hand. Asuna hesitantly stashed her weapon as well and took the hand.

The other girl stretched her shoulders wide, the bodily command to deploy wings. The translucent, batlike wings popped out and propelled her into the air.

"Um, hang on." Asuna hastily spread her shoulder blades and leaped into flight. Yuuki grinned and turned, still holding Asuna's hand, then shot upward like a rocket.

"Wait! Where are you going, Asuna?!" came a high-pitched voice. Asuna looked down as she was hurtled upward and saw Lisbeth, hand to her mouth, looking both shocked and annoyed. Leafa, Silica, and Yui—who was sitting atop Kirito's head—all looked stunned, but the black-clad spriggan was grinning as though he expected something like this to happen.

Bolstered by his expression, Asuna smiled back and sucked in a deep breath.

"Uh, um...I'll get in touch later!" she yelled to Lisbeth, just as Yuuki's wings glowed purple and burst into a dash. Asuna desperately beat her wings to keep up with the force yanking her onward, in the trail of the mysterious warrior.

Yuuki headed directly south over the lake that covered the twenty-fourth floor and plunged straight through the outer aperture of Aincrad, breaking out beyond the flying castle.

"Pwah!"

A mass of thick, wet cloud hit Asuna's face. After several seconds of flying straight through whiteness, the clouds gave way, and there was an infinity of cerulean blue around them.

Far below and straight ahead, there was a green cone piercing the clouds—the foliage of the World Tree that loomed over the center of Alfheim. Directly below that, barely visible, was the faded blue surface of the earth. Based on the round, carved coastline and the circular island floating in the water, Aincrad seemed to be flying over Crescent Bay, the home of the undines.

Just as Asuna started to wonder where they were going, Yuuki made a sudden ninety-degree turn directly upward.

She was faced with the looming sheer cliff that was the outside of Aincrad, several dozen feet away. As they climbed, they cut across floor after floor, each one three hundred feet tall, but the Absolute Sword kept pushing upward.

Even with the power of flight, they could only freely enter those floors that had already been conquered. Above that, the outer apertures were solid, inviolable space. Asuna began to worry and opened her mouth to check, but just as she had taken a fresh breath, they turned ninety degrees yet again.

Yuuki was heading for the twenty-seventh floor. If Asuna's memory was correct, that was the current player frontier. They shot through the mossy outside and plunged into the interior, everything suddenly growing darker.

The twenty-seventh floor of Aincrad was a land of eternal night. The outer apertures were extremely narrow, so barely any sunlight got inside, even at midday. On the inside, craggy rock mountains stretched all the way to the ceiling above, and enormous hexagonal pillars of crystal grew out of the ground, emitting pale blue light. It was rather similar in atmosphere to the underground gnome world at the northern end of Alfheim.

The imp girl, who would have the second-best night vision behind a spriggan, pulled Asuna along through the rocks. At times, flocks of flying gargoyle monsters appeared ahead, but Yuuki skillfully evaded their search capabilities.

Eventually, they plunged into a deep valley and flew at low speed until a small town nestled into the circular valley came into view: Rombal, the main city of the twenty-seventh floor.

The town seemed to be scooped right out of the rock, a complex system of narrow alleys and staircases that was lit by orange lamps. It was an oddly soothing sight, like a little glowing fire in the midst of the dark of night.

Yuuki and Asuna forged trails of purple and blue as they descended gently toward the circular plaza at the center of the town. Soft BGM began to play in their ears, the sign that they had entered the safe haven of civilization, and their noses were tickled by the faint scent of stew as their heels landed on the paving stone.

Asuna let out a long breath and surveyed her surroundings. Rombal was meant to be a town of night spirits, and as a result, there were no larger buildings present. There were only numerous quaint workshops, businesses and inns crammed in tight, carved out of bluish stone and lit by orange lamps. The contrast gave it an eerie beauty and the bustling feeling of a night festival.

In the days of the old *SAO*, the floor gave the player population trouble, but without any notable features or facilities, they didn't have much reason to spend time there. She only remembered staying there a few days, at best. But as the current frontier of progress in New Aincrad, it was currently bustling with players, each bristling with impressive gear. Every face on the street gave off the impression of a hardened warrior with more than a little eccentricity, and the sight filled Asuna with both nostalgia and bitterness.

She had raced through the floors up until the twenty-second, just for the sake of buying that forest cabin, but Asuna had hardly participated in any of the boss fights since then. The catharsis of opening new towns was better meant for those new players who hadn't experienced it before, and being among the frontline players did not always bring up the most enjoyable memories for her.

She shut her eyes and shook her head to clear out the past, then looked to the Absolute Sword nearby.

"So…why did you bring me here? Is there something important in this town?" she asked. The imp girl grinned and took her hand again.

"First, I want to introduce you to my companions! This way!"

"Er, wait…"

Asuna had to chase after the racing girl, who plunged down one of the narrow alleys that extended in a radial pattern outward from the plaza. They went up a small stairway, then down one, then over a bridge, then through a tunnel, emerging at last in front of a small building. They walked through the door, under a cast-iron hanging sign fashioned into a cauldron shape, reading INN. Inside, they passed a napping, whiskered old NPC at the front desk and went into the pub in the rear.

"Welcome back, Yuuki! Any luck this time?!" came an excited boy's voice as they entered the room.

Five players were seated around a circular table in the center of the pub. There were no others in the room. Yuuki strode over to them and turned back to Asuna. She flourished toward the group and proudly announced, "Allow me to introduce you to the members of my guild, the Sleeping Knights."

She made another half turn and pointed to Asuna. "And this lady is, um…"

Yuuki paused. She ducked her head a bit, rolled her big eyes, and stuck out her tongue impishly. "Sorry…I didn't actually ask her name yet."

The five players sitting around the table all groaned and slumped theatrically in their chairs. Asuna couldn't help but giggle. "Nice to meet you. I'm Asuna."

Suddenly, the small salamander boy sitting on the left leaped up, his orange ponytail waving. "I'm Jun! Nice to meet you, Asuna!" he blurted.

Next to him was a large gnome. The narrowed eyes below his unruly, sandy locks added a touch of charm to his imposing bulk. He tried to suck in his bulging stomach and bowed, slowly adding, "Er, um, my name is Tecchi. It's a pleasure."

Next to stand was a young, thin leprechaun. His neatly parted, bronzy-blond hair combined with metal-frame glasses to give him the look of a student. His small, round eyes went wide and he bent over, blushing for some reason.

"M-my name is, um, Talken, and it's, um, n-n-nice to…*Ow!!*"

The woman sitting to his left kicked him hard in the shin with a heavy boot. "Get over that stammering habit, Tal! You do it every time you meet a girl."

The owner of that forceful voice stood up, scraping her chair against the floor. She gave Asuna a full-faced grin and scrunched up her flared mane. "I'm Nori. Good to meet you, Asuna."

Based on her tanned skin and gray wings, she seemed to be a spriggan, but the heavy brows, sharp eyes, and heavyset figure did not seem to match the wispy, illusionist spriggan race.

The last was an undine, like Asuna. Her shoulder-length hair was an aqua so pale it was nearly white, and her long eyelashes hid gentle eyes that were nearly navy. She had a long-bridged nose, small lips, and a surprisingly fragile-looking body: perfectly fitting for the race that was meant to be healers.

The woman stood gracefully and, in a smooth, calm voice, intoned, "It is nice to meet you. I am Siune. Thank you for coming."

"And," said the Absolute Sword, jumping onto the end of the line, her amethyst eyes sparkling, "I'm Yuuki, the leader of the guild! Asuna..." She took big strides over and grabbed both of Asuna's hands. "Let's do our best together!"

"Um...and what are we doing?" Asuna asked, a smile frozen on her face.

Yuuki looked stunned for a second, then stuck out her tongue again. "Oh, right. I didn't explain anything yet!"

Flop! The five at the table slumped in their chairs again, and Asuna couldn't hold in her laughter this time. She clutched her sides and chuckled, and eventually Yuuki and the others joined in with booming laughter.

Asuna took another look at the Sleeping Knights, trying to stifle her giggles, and felt something shiver up and down her back.

All of them were tremendous players. She could tell, just from watching each and every limb move. All six of them were completely comfortable with controlling their avatars in a full-dive environment. She was certain that with their weapons, they were each close to the Absolute Sword in skill.

Asuna—and, she suspected, Kirito and the others—was completely unaware that there had been such a crack team of veteran players in the game. If they had all come from another VRMMO like Yuuki, they must have been quite a legendary guild in their old haunt. She wondered what would make them abandon their familiar avatars and carefully acquired items and move to *ALO*...

At last, Yuuki got over her giggles and scratched at the red headband, noting regretfully, "I'm sorry, Asuna. I brought you all the way here without explaining why. I got so happy to find someone else as strong as me that I just got carried away...Well, allow me to ask properly. Help me...I mean, help *us!*"

"Help...you?" Asuna repeated, confused. A number of thoughts ran through her mind.

It probably wasn't a request to join their party to help them get more money, items, or skill points. A guild with this much man-power wasn't going to be much different with Asuna added.

At the same time, it was hard to imagine they needed help get-ting a certain item or buying a house. Unlike the old *SAO*, where information was traded for exorbitant prices, *ALO* had plenty of third-party websites that offered all the game info you could ever need, for free. By consulting those sites, resourceful players could get just about any items they wanted.

Perhaps what Yuuki saw in Asuna was not just numerical strength, but the entirety of knowledge that went into mastering battle. Yet it was PvP play that needed that skill the most, not PvE monster hunting. And since it involved a guild invitation, per-haps what the Absolute Sword planned wasn't duels like on that little island, but a major group battle—a massive slaughter with some other guild, no rules involved.

Asuna mulled it over, bit her lip, then said, "Um...if it involves helping you in a war with some other guild, then I'm sorry, but..."

Player-versus-player fights that didn't happen within the struc-tured tournament system or some other rule set always left her with unresolved emotions afterward. Naturally, it was a minor-ity of players who held a long-term grudge over a momentary competition, but she couldn't discount the possibility that such actions might end up causing trouble not just for herself but for her friends.

For that reason, even if she suffered boorish, unfair behavior from others out in the hunting grounds, she made sure never to draw her sword on another player.

Asuna opened her mouth, ready to explain her philosophy as briefly as she could, but Yuuki gave her a wide-eyed shake of her head.

"No, no, we're not going to war or anything. It's, um…well… You might laugh at us, but…"

She looked down, mumbling shyly, then looked up at Asuna and admitted, unexpectedly, "The thing is…we want to beat the boss of this floor."

"H-huh?!" Asuna stammered. That was not at all what she expected. She had been anticipating something even more grandiose and extreme than a guild war, and instead got the most orthodox answer of all: beating a floor boss. It was the exact same thing that just about every other player on this floor had to be thinking.

"When you say…'boss,' you mean the kind at the end of the labyrinth…? Not some kind of timed mob with a unique name?" she asked, just to be sure. Yuuki nodded.

"Yep, exactly. The kind you can only beat once."

"Hmm…I see, a boss…"

Asuna looked at the other five members of the guild, whose eyes were shining as they awaited her answer. It seemed as though Yuuki's team wanted to be counted among the "advancement guilds" who specialized in defeating bosses to push the player base's progress onward. Freshly converted with no personal connections, they wanted instruction from Asuna to help them join the ranks of the game's expert players—perhaps.

"Well…given how good you are, Abso…I mean, Yuuki…"

After much surprised blinking and a few attempts to switch her mind into gear, Asuna pondered the practical possibility of the request. At present, the frontline players working on Aincrad were about 80 percent *ALO* veterans and 20 percent comeback players from the original *SAO*. For now, the two groups were meshed together, with many guilds featuring a combination of

ALO and *SAO* types, but shortly after the Aincrad update, relations were stiff. After all, they each had their pride: The "fairies" were playing the oldest game for the AmuSphere, while the "swordsmen" had played the very first VRMMO in existence. Asuna was much the same way.

If a group of converted players from a different game barged in and asked to join the raid, their prospects might not be great, but Yuuki the Absolute Sword was the kind of off-the-charts power that created exceptions. If the other five were equivalent to her, they just needed a chance to display that talent.

"Let's see...I understand they've mapped out this floor's labyrinth up close to the boss chamber, so I can't make any guarantees about getting a spot on this raid party, but as long as you start off by participating on the next floor, they might see the merit in allowing you to join the raid...But the maximum member count for a raid is forty-nine, so I can't be sure they'll make room for all six of you, either," Asuna explained. Yuuki shrank back shyly a bit, and once again she blew the top off of Asuna's expectations.

"Um, well, that's not exactly what I mean. I don't want to join a big team...I want to defeat the boss with just the seven of us."

"...Wh-whaaat?!"

Asuna's shriek was the loudest noise that had echoed off the walls since she arrived in the pub.

The reason was quite simple.

Compared to the boss monsters that loomed over each floor in the original *SAO*, the New Aincrad bosses were considerably stronger. What with the changes in the game's system, it wasn't such a simple comparison, but given that with proper strategy and planning, the old bosses could be defeated without losing a single player, it was telling that the new bosses scattered their human foes like dandelion fuzz with ultrapowerful standard attacks and unique moves.

That necessitated changes in battle strategy, of course. A raid party needed close to the maximum number of members, and more healers were needed to stem the tide of deaths. Rather than having one member sacrifice himself to deal ten damage, get ten members to safely and reliably deal eleven. Asuna was participating in the boss battles up to the twenty-first floor, and even at those low floors, the number of 7x7 raid parties with the full forty-nine members that ended up completely wiped out was uncountable.

Naturally, the bosses got tougher as the floors went on. The recent Christmas update unlocked the floors in the latter twenties, but the twenty-sixth floor below them had taken the best and brightest of several major guilds to clear.

So no matter how powerful Yuuki's little guild might be, adding Asuna to bring them to a total of seven wasn't going to make a bit of difference against the boss. She tried to explain that to the girl as simply as possible, choosing her words carefully.

"...and that's why...I don't think having just seven of us is going to work..."

When she finished, the Sleeping Knights looked among one another and smiled shyly for some reason. Yuuki spoke for the group.

"Yeah, it didn't work at all. We tried it on the twenty-fifth- and twenty-sixth-floor bosses already."

"What?! The...the six of you?!"

"Yep. We really did pretty well, in my opinion...but we couldn't get enough MP and healing potions to do the trick. While we were trying out different strategies and load outs, a bigger group came along and beat them each time."

"Oh, I see...So you are taking this seriously." Asuna examined the six faces again.

It was certainly a reckless and pointless attempt, but she had nothing against that sort of pluck. Once players were fully familiar with a game, they became too set in their knowledge of what they could and couldn't do. The spirit of ambition that pulsed through the Sleeping Knights was very fresh and exciting to Asuna—and familiar, as well.

"But...why? Why do you want to beat the boss on your own, rather than with other guilds?"

Of course, beating a boss with so few members would result in an absurd amount of yrd and exclusive loot for each person. But that didn't seem like a motive that fit the people she'd just met.

"Um, well...um, well," Yuuki chattered, her amethyst eyes wide. But the words did not come. Her mouth opened and shut in hesitation as she tried to find the right way to describe their plan.

That was when the tall undine named Siune came to Yuuki's aid. "I will explain. But first, please be seated."

Once all seven of them were sitting at the table and had received an order of drinks from the NPC waitress, Siune neatly folded her long fingers and began her explanation.

"As you might have surmised already, we did not meet in this realm. We were part of an online community that had nothing to do with games...and found that we all got along quite well. We've been friends for about...two years now."

She paused to reflect on the past, her eyes downcast.

"They are the most wonderful companions. We have traveled to various worlds and gone on many adventures together. But unfortunately, it's only through the spring that we're likely to be able to continue. Everyone is going to be...busy after that. So before we break up the team, we decided that we wanted to make one last, unforgettable memory together. Out of the countless VRMMO worlds out there, we looked for the most enjoyable, beautiful, and exhilarating world, so that we could work to achieve some grand goal together. After converting to various games, we eventually arrived here."

Siune looked around the group in turn. Jun, Tecchi, Talken, Nori, and Yuuki each nodded, their faces shining. Siune smiled wanly and continued. "We have found that Alfheim, land of fairies, and its floating castle Aincrad, make for a splendid place. The beautiful cities, forests, plains, the World Tree, and this castle—none of us will ever forget our memories of flying together here.

If there's one more thing we want…it's to leave some trace of ourselves in this world."

Beneath her half-closed lids, Siune's navy blue eyes took on a light of intent. "If we defeat a floor boss, our names will be left on the Monument of Swordsmen found in Blackiron Palace on the first floor, I understand."

"Ah…"

Asuna went wide-eyed, then nodded. It was true that the names of the players who defeated bosses were recorded in Blackiron Palace. Asuna herself was listed in the twenty-first-floor slot.

"Well…it's only for stroking our own egos, but we really want to have our names on that monument. There's just one problem. If a single party beats the boss, all of their names are written down, but if the group is multiple parties, only the party leaders' names are recorded."

"Oh…I see. Yes, you're right about that," Asuna said, recalling the interior of the palace.

The Monument of Swordsmen was a 3-D object modeled in the game's physical space, which meant it naturally had a limited area—certainly not enough for the names of every player to participate in boss battles up to the hundredth floor. There were only seven slots for each floor. So as Siune said, if a single party beat the boss, all their names could fit, but if it were a full raid, only the seven party leaders would be represented.

Once Siune was certain that Asuna had picked up on their intention, she continued. "In other words, for all the members of the Sleeping Knights to show up on the monument, we must defeat the boss with just a single party. We did our best on the twenty-fifth and twenty-sixth floors, but we just couldn't get over the top…So we came to a group decision. The maximum size of a party is seven, so we had room for one more. Presumptuous as it may sound, we wanted someone even stronger than Yuuki, the best of our guild, so that we could ask him or her to join us in our task."

"I see…So that's what's going on," Asuna said, letting out

the breath she'd been holding. She looked down at the white tablecloth.

Leaving their names on the Monument of Swordsmen. I understand that desire.

Because all online games—not just VRMMOs—demanded plenty of time from their players, many people withdrew from them in the spring, when the Japanese school year ended and people looked for new jobs. It was an eventuality that even close-knit guilds that had been together for years would one day break apart. So it was natural to want to leave behind traces of that bond for as long as the game world existed.

For her part, Asuna didn't know how long she'd be able to play *ALO*. If her mother got any tougher on her, she might take away the AmuSphere. So if her remaining time was limited, then she wanted to make each and every second count, just like they did.

"...What do you say? Will you accept? We converted here not long ago, so I'm afraid we're not in a position to offer you much..."

Siune opened a trade window in order to present a money amount. Asuna cut her off immediately.

"Er, no, it's going to cost quite a bit to undertake the task, so you should keep what money you have for that. As long as I get something from the boss, that should be fine..."

"Then you'll accept?!"

The faces of Siune and her five companions sparkled. As she looked at each of them in turn, Asuna felt herself secretly wondering how it had come to this. It had only started with a little spark of curiosity about the mysterious Absolute Sword. And suddenly she was here, all the way at the front line, far from their dueling spot, introduced to a group of friends, and accepting an invitation to tackle the floor boss together. It hadn't even been an hour yet.

Asuna stared into the amethyst eyes of Yuuki as they glittered with expectation—the very person who had dragged her into this roller coaster of events. It was too sudden, and too forceful, but such strange encounters were one of the joys of a VRMMO. And most important, there was a faint but certain feeling brewing inside of her: She could sense that she would get along with this odd duelist and her companions.

"Umm…Just give me a bit of time."

It was for that reason that she didn't want to take this decision lightly. Asuna sucked in a deep breath, fixed her eyes on the cups on the table, and tried to calm down her slightly bewildered thoughts into a rational state. She set aside her confusion and surprise, focusing just on the grand goal of Yuuki's team.

Long ago, Asuna had led the charge against several boss monsters as the sub-leader of a guild that no longer existed.

She spent hours with other advanced guilds and solo players, arguing and screaming about attack patterns and weaknesses, even getting to her knees to beg for help when they were short on manpower. The reason she went to such lengths was to uphold an ironclad rule that existed in that world: not to allow a single fatality.

But now, everything had changed. In the land of fairies, the only rule every player had to follow was to enjoy themselves. Would it be "enjoyable" to admit you stood no chance and give up before trying? Yuuki's guild had tried two boss monsters and acquitted themselves well, even as a tiny team of six.

Rather than worrying about likely failure and overthinking, she ought to try it out. It felt like forever since she'd played so recklessly. What was the worst that could happen? Only the loss of a few experience points each.

"…Let's get as far as we can—setting aside our chances of success." Asuna smirked mischievously, raising her head. Instantly, Yuuki's adorable face burst into sunshine. The five companions raised a cheer, and she leaned over the table to squeeze Asuna's outstretched hand in both of hers.

"Thank you, Miss Asuna! I had a feeling you'd say that from the first moment our blades struck!"

"Just call me Asuna," she replied with a grin, which Yuuki returned.

"And call me Yuuki!"

*   *   *

Once she had shaken hands with each of the overly eager members at the table and they'd toasted with another round of mugs, Asuna turned to Yuuki and brought up something that came to her mind.

"By the way, Yuuki…you were looking for powerful people to duel, right?"

"Yeah, that's right."

"Well, there must have been other good fighters before me. Do you happen to remember a spriggan dressed in black with a longsword? I'm guessing that he would be a much bigger help to you than me…"

"Ohh…" That seemed to be enough to remind Yuuki of Kirito right away. She nodded but frowned, crossing her arms. "Yes, I remember. He was tough!"

"Then…why didn't you ask him to join you?"

"Hmm…"

It was rare for Yuuki not to have an immediate answer. She put on a distracted smile.

"He's not right for us."

"Wh…why?"

"He realized my secret."

Yuuki and the others didn't seem to want to talk about that, so Asuna couldn't press further. She assumed the "secret" had to have something to do with her Absolute Sword strength, but whatever Kirito had noticed, Asuna couldn't begin to guess.

Suddenly, the leprechaun Talken spoke up to change the topic, pushing his round glasses higher onto his nose.

"So…as far as concrete plans to beat the boss…Wh-where do we start?"

"Ah…well…"

Asuna took a deep swig from her mug of fruit-flavored beverage to smooth the doubt in her throat, and then held up a finger.

"The first and most important thing is to have clear knowledge of the boss's attack patterns. If everyone evades when you need to evade, defends when you need to defend, and attacks like crazy when it's time to attack, we might just stand a chance. The problem is how to gain that information…I don't suppose it will work to ask the bigger guilds that focus on taking down bosses. I think it'll be necessary to give it a preliminary attempt, with the expectation of failure."

"Yeah, we'll be fine with that! The problem is, on the last floor, and the one before that, we went in unprepared and lost, and then another guild won right after that," Yuuki noted sadly. On the other side of the table, Jun the salamander frowned, his spiky eyebrows folding together.

"We went back to it just three hours later, and it was already over. Maybe it's just my imagination, but…it was like they were waiting for us to fail…"

"Ahh," said Asuna, putting her hand to her mouth to think.

She'd heard rumors about various confrontations surrounding boss fights recently. Usually it was about the bigger guilds trying to run everything, but would they really bother to pay attention to a measly six-man party? Still, some information couldn't be ignored.

"Well, in that case, we should be well prepared and expect to retry it as soon as possible if we wipe once. What time would be most convenient for everyone?"

"Oh, sorry. Talken and I can't do nights. How about one o'clock tomorrow afternoon?" said Nori, the well-built spriggan, scratching her head apologetically.

"Yeah, that works for me. Shall we meet at this inn at one tomorrow, then?"

The Sleeping Knights each offered a comment of agreement. Asuna looked at the group and energetically cried, "Let's give it our best!"

At last, Asuna left the inn, patting Yuuki's shoulder as the excited girl thanked her yet again, looking sad as she left. She decided the first step was to return to her group of friends. She trotted back to the teleport gate in the center of Rombal, gleefully imagining how shocked they would be when she explained all that had happened.

She navigated the streets as best she could on shaky memory, and had finally emerged in the bustling circular plaza—when something odd happened.

With the suddenness of a switch being flipped, the world went black. Asuna was plunged into darkness without sight or sound.

4

There was a sudden falling sensation, like she'd been hurled into a bottomless pit.

Suddenly, her sense of up and down shifted ninety degrees, and she felt a powerful pressure on her back. Next, Asuna tensed against the shock of each of her five senses violently reconnecting and resuming.

After a few eyelid twitches, she was able to pry teary eyes open to see the ceiling of her room. At last, the familiar softness of her bed registered on her skin. As she breathed, quick and short, the chaos of her senses finally began to subside.

What had happened? It could have been a momentary power outage or an issue with the AmuSphere. She took a deep breath at last and sensed the scent of a perfume that did not belong to her. She sat up, suspicion sinking in, and her mouth fell open.

Standing right next to her bed with a stern expression, holding a thin gray power cord in her hand, was Asuna's mother. She had pulled the power directly out of the AmuSphere Asuna was wearing.

In other words, the abnormal disconnection was the result of Kyouko powering off the AmuSphere. "Wh-what was that for, Mother?!" Asuna protested.

But Kyouko only glanced silently at the north wall, her expression severe. Asuna followed her gaze and saw the hands of the wall clock indicating that it was about five minutes past six thirty. Her mouth twitched in surprise.

Kyouko said, "I told you when you were late to dinner last month—the next time you're late because of this game, I'm going to pull the plug."

Her tone was beyond cold, almost gloating. Asuna nearly shouted back at her. She looked down to stifle that urge and managed to emit, low and trembling, "It's my fault for forgetting the time. But you didn't have to pull out the cord. If you shook my body or shouted at my ear, it would send a warning inside to me..."

"The last time I did that, it took you five minutes to wake up."

"That's because...I had to travel, and say good-bye, and..."

"Good-bye? You're prioritizing simple pleasantries in that nonsensical game over actual arrangements in real life? Don't you care about the hard work that our help put into the meal, only for you to let it go cold?"

A number of arguments ran through Asuna's head. *Even in a game, they're still real people. Besides, when you go work at your school, you routinely waste an entire day's worth of cooking with a single phone call.* But she only looked down again, sighing a trembling breath. Her eventual response was short and simple.

"...I'm sorry. I'll be careful next time."

"There won't be a next time. The next time you let this thing ruin your actual responsibilities, I'll take it away. Besides." Kyouko sneered, glaring at the AmuSphere still attached to Asuna's forehead. "I just don't understand you anymore. That bizarre contraption has cost you two precious years of your life, don't you understand? Why doesn't it make you sick just to look at it?"

"This one isn't like the NerveGear," Asuna mumbled. She took the double-ringed circle off her head. After the lessons of the *SAO* Incident, the AmuSphere was constructed with several safety mechanisms to prevent that from happening again, but Asuna recognized that it would be pointless to say so. Besides, it was true that, different device or not, Asuna had been in a vegetative state for two years because of a VRMMO game. Her mother must have been worried sick during that time, and both of her parents probably steeled themselves for her eventual death. She understood why the woman would hate the device.

Her mother sighed in response to Asuna's silence and turned for the door.

"It's time to eat. Get changed and come down at once."

"…I'm not hungry today."

It wasn't fair to Akiyo the housekeeper, who cooked dinner, but she was in no mood to sit across from her mother and eat now.

"As you wish," Kyouko responded, shaking her head as she left. When the door clicked shut, Asuna reached for the room control panel and set it to vent, hoping to drive out the scent of her mother's eau de toilette. Instead, it persistently hung in the air.

The excitement she'd felt about meeting Yuuki the Absolute Sword and her wonderful friends, and the anticipation of a new adventure with them, had melted like a snowball in the hot sun. Asuna stood up and opened the closet, slipping on a pair of damaged jeans with ripped knees. Next was a thick cotton parka and a white down jacket on top of that. They were some of the few clothes in her possession that weren't chosen for her by her mother.

She straightened her hair and grabbed a bag and her cell phone before leaving the room. She got down the stairs and slipped on her sneakers at the front door when the security panel at the door screeched, "Asuna! Where are you going at this time of night?!"

Asuna ignored her and opened the door before her mother could remotely lock it. The instant the double doors opened, metal security bolts shot out from both sides, but Asuna slipped through them just in time. The damp, cold night air struck her face.

Only once she had crossed the driveway and escaped the property through the walk-in entrance to the side of the front gate did Asuna let out the breath she'd been holding. The vapor turned white before her eyes before dissipating into the air. She pulled the jacket zipper up to her neck and stuck her hands into her pockets, then started walking for the Miyanosaka station of the Tokyu Setagaya line.

She didn't have a destination in mind. She'd run out of the house in an act of rebellion against her mother, but even Asuna knew it was just a pointless bit of childish posturing. The phone in her jeans pocket had a GPS tracker, so her mother knew where she was at all times—not that Asuna had the courage to leave her phone behind. That frustration with her own weakness only amplified the feeling of powerlessness in her chest.

Asuna stopped in front of a children's park at the end of a row of large mansions. She sat down on the reverse U-shaped piece of metal pipe blocking the entrance of the park and pulled her phone out of her pocket.

She traced the screen with a finger, bringing up "Kirito"— Kazuto's contact info from her address book. Her finger hovered over the CALL button, but Asuna held it there, shutting her eyes.

She wanted to call him and tell him to come pick her up on his motorcycle with an extra helmet. She wanted to sit on the back of that tiny, noisy, oddly speedy vehicle with her arms clenched around his midsection, riding straight along the major roads empty in the wake of the holiday. Just like flying at top speed in Alfheim, that would certainly clear the cobwebs out of her mind.

But if she saw Kazuto now, she would lose control of her emotions and break down into sobs, revealing all the things she wanted to keep secret from him. Her forced transfer from their school. The possibility that she might not be able to play *ALO* anymore. The cold reality that pushed her in a direction that had been erected for her since birth, and her inability to fight against it—in other words, her own weakness, which she had tried to keep hidden.

She moved her finger away from the screen and held the SLEEP button instead. After a brief squeeze of the phone, she put it back into her pocket.

Asuna wanted to be stronger. To have the strength of will to never waver in her decisions. The strength to proceed in the direction that she desired, without relying on someone else to take care of her.

But at the same time, a voice screamed that it wanted to be weaker. The weakness to not hide her true self, to cry when she wanted to cry. The weakness to cling, to cry out for protection and help.

A snowflake landed on her cheek and melted into water. Asuna looked up, silently watching the faint blots of light as they descended from the pale gloom of night.

5

"So basically, Yuuki, Jun, and Tecchi will be the forwards, Talken and Nori will be midrange, and Siune will be the backup."

Asuna examined the lineup of the Sleeping Knights with their equipment on display, a finger to her chin. When she'd been introduced to them last night, they were all in their light ordinary wear, but now they were outfitted with powerful ancient weapons.

Yuuki had on her black half armor and longsword, like the day before. Jun the salamander was wearing a blazing bronze full plate that seemed out of place on his petite frame, and there was a greatsword on his back that nearly matched him in height.

Tecchi the enormous gnome also had thick plate armor, as well as a tower shield like a door. His weapon was a heavy mace with menacing protrusions on all sides.

The bespectacled leprechaun Talken's slender build was covered in brassy light armor, and his weapon was a frightfully long spear. Next to him, the imposing lady spriggan Nori wore a loose cloth *dogi* without any metal, to go with a steel quarterstaff that nearly reached the ceiling.

And Siune the undine, the only mage of the group, wore a priestly cassock of white and navy blue, with a round, puffy hat like a brioche bun and a thin silver rod in her right hand. It was a well-balanced party on the whole, but they were a bit under-served when it came to buffing and healing.

"So it looks like I ought to take a support role," Asuna noted, loosening her sword belt to exchange her rapier for a magic-boosting wand.

Yuuki shrugged apologetically. "Sorry, Asuna. It's a shame to put you in the back, when you're so good with the sword."

"No, it's fine. I wouldn't be good as a shield, anyway. Instead, Jun and Tecchi will have to get whacked a lot, so be prepared!"

She looked at the two heavy warriors with a smirk. The sala-mander and gnome looked at each other, their sizes incredibly mismatched, then smacked their breastplates in unison.

"Y-yeah! We're on top of it!" Jun said enthusiastically, if a bit awkwardly. Everyone laughed.

The date was Thursday, January 8th, 2026.

At one o'clock on the last day of winter vacation, Asuna had shown up at the same inn in Rombal, main town of the twenty-seventh floor, to rejoin the Sleeping Knights as promised. They were ready to test out the boss monster that presided over the top floor of the labyrinth tower.

Asuna understood that her role here was less to boost their numerical strength and more to provide strategic advice that would make the most of everyone's abilities. In terms of sheer power, every one of the Sleeping Knights was probably Asuna's superior. The one thing she had that they didn't was knowledge and experience of this game.

The first step was examining everyone's build and gear to establish a basic party archetype.

Now that she knew she'd be in the back line, Asuna opened her inventory and dropped her rapier inside, replacing it with her wand. It was a cheap-looking item, not much more than a branch with a single leaf at the end, but in reality, it was taken from the very top of the World Tree. She had to evade the furious attacks of a mammoth guardian dragon to get it.

"Now," Asuna started, twirling the wand in her fingertips, "let's go check out that boss chamber!"

The group of seven left the inn and flew into the eternal night sky.

As she would have expected, they were all expert flyers without the need of flight-stick assistance. Asuna marveled at the smoothness of their ascent; they didn't seem to be freshly converted to *ALO* in the least. But that wasn't so much caused by a familiarity with the genre as it was an intimate understanding of the full-dive tech that made VRMMOs possible. True, a scant handful of players were like this, but in her long history, Asuna could count those she knew on one hand, led by Kirito.

So having six of them together at once made her wonder how such a guild got formed. In a logical sense, being January 8th, this was the time most people in society were getting back to work or school. Asuna's school was confident enough in its curriculum that she didn't have to start the third term until tomorrow. However, getting all six of them available in the middle of the day at once would normally be very difficult to schedule.

Given their absurd strength, among other things, the most likely answer was that they were all extremely hardcore players. But Asuna felt that was not the case. Asuna did not get that sense of bristling pride from the Sleeping Knights that was exuded by most guilds consisting of such members. It seemed that they were all purely enjoying the game on its own merits.

Asuna almost never gave any thought to the real players behind the avatars in-game, but she couldn't help but wonder now. Meanwhile, up ahead, Yuuki shouted, "I can see the labyrinth!"

She looked up with a start and caught sight of a huge tower beyond the line of rocky mountains. The circular structure ran from the ground straight up to the bottom of the floor above. A number of hexagonal crystal pillars, each the size of a small house, jutted from the base, their faint blue glow dimly illuminating the tower in the darkness. The entrance yawned black and forbidding at the foot of the building.

They hovered outside to make sure there were no monsters or parties loitering around the entrance. She had already announced the plan for today's spontaneous boss attempt to Lisbeth and the others, of course. They were surprised by the Absolute Sword's sudden request, but she was relieved to hear them all pledge to chip in. Of course, the point of all this was to make one last big memory for Yuuki and her guild, so they couldn't turn it into too big of a thing. Asuna's friends decided to give them all the healing potions they could carry and wished them well.

Ever since the start, Kirito had maintained a knowing, meaningful silence about the other girl. While he did seem to temporarily fall into a meditative state, he still saw her off with a smile, and he convinced Yui that it was better to remain behind with him. In a sense, helping another guild was a form of betrayal, so Asuna was grateful that her friends were so understanding. This thought warmed her heart as she trailed in the back row of the team during their descent to the tower.

They landed on dark soil and stared up at the massive edifice. She'd looked up these pillars dozens of times since starting the old *SAO*, always tipping her head back to inevitably gaze at the floor above, but when up close at ground level—rather than observing from the air— their tremendous size never failed to make her feel insignificant.

"So...as we decided, we'll try to avoid combat with ordinary monsters as much as possible on the way," Asuna declared. Yuuki and the others nodded back, their faces grim. The party theatrically drew its weapons from waist and back alike.

Siune, the magically inclined undine, raised her silver rod and began to chant a series of buffing spells. Various visual effects surrounded the seven party members, and a number of status icons popped into life beneath their HP bars, at the upper left of their view. Next, Nori the spriggan cast a spell that gave everyone night vision. Asuna knew a few status spells, too, but Siune's skill levels were higher.

Once the preparations were complete, they all indicated their readiness with a nod, and Yuuki set foot inside the labyrinth.

It started off as a natural cave, but once the walls and floor switched to manmade paving stones, the temperature of the air dropped, and dampness clung to their skin. As she remembered from the *SAO* days, the interior of the labyrinth was vexingly large, and the monsters were much tougher than those found outside. Plus, like those dungeons down in Alfheim below, there was no flying allowed inside. They'd bought map data ahead of time from an info dealer, but even then, it would take a good three hours to reach the boss chamber.

Or so I'd expected.

Instead, just an hour into the journey, they stood in a massive corridor that led to a set of enormous chamber doors at its end. Asuna could only marvel at the strength of Yuuki and her companions. She had an idea of their strengths individually, but what made them even better was the precision of their teamwork. They didn't need words; just a tiny bit of body language would send the signal to stop or proceed as necessary. Asuna was fine just tagging along in the back row. They only got into three battles on the way, and they followed her instructions by dispatching the leader first, throwing the others into confusion, and allowing the party to slip past and evade further trouble.

As they headed down the corridor to the chamber doors, Asuna couldn't resist the urge to lean over and mutter into Siune's ear. "I dunno…was my presence really necessary? It almost seems like there's nothing I can do to make you guys any better…"

Siune went wide-eyed and shook her head dramatically. "No, don't say that. It was thanks to you that we didn't fall into a single trap and avoided so much combat. The last two attempts, we took on every battle, so we were quite drained by the time we got this far…"

"W-well, that's an incredible feat in and of itself…Oh, wait, Yuuki," Asuna called out. The three at the front came to a halt. They'd already covered half of the long hallway to the door, close enough for the gruesome reliefs carved into the doors to be visible. There were pillars at regular intervals on either side of the hallway, but there were no monsters in sight, not even hiding in the shadows.

Yuuki and Jun looked back at her questioningly. Asuna put a finger to her lips to hush them, then stared beyond the last pillar on the left side of the massive doors. The only illumination in the corridor came from pale flames glowing from niches set high on the pillars. Even with the help of Nori's night-vision magic, it was hard to sense the fine movement of the shadows flickering against the stone walls. But something in Asuna's instincts said there was an anomaly in her vision.

She waved the others back and raised her wand, chanting long spell-words as quickly as she could and holding her free hand up in front of her. When the chant was done, five little fish appeared above her hand, their pectoral fins as long as wings. She leaned over the transparent blue fish and blew softly in the direction of the wall.

The fish leaped off of her hand and began to swim straight through the air. She had summoned "searchers" that would undo the effects of concealing magic. The five swam in a narrowly splayed wave, until two of them eventually plunged into the wavering of the air that Asuna had sensed.

Blue light spread at once. The searchers vanished, and the veil of green air that they had revealed began to dissolve.

"Ah!" Yuuki exclaimed in surprise. On the other side of the pillar, where there had been nothing before, three players suddenly appeared.

Asuna's eyes quickly scanned the three. Two imps and one sylph, all equipped with light daggers. But their equipment grade was high. She didn't recognize their faces, but she did recognize the guild tag on their cursors: a side-facing horse on a shield. It was the symbol of a major guild that had been tackling the labyrinth towers since the twenty-third floor.

It was a bad sign that they were hiding in a stretch of labyrinth without any monsters. That was a PK tactic. Asuna raised her wand, preparing for long-range attacks from afar, while the rest of the party brandished their weapons in turn.

But to their surprise, one of the trio raised a hand in panic and shrieked, "Stop, stop! We don't mean to fight!"

The pressing note in the voice didn't sound faked, but Asuna wasn't going to let her guard down yet. She shouted back, "Then put away your weapons!"

The three shared a look and returned their daggers to their sheaths. Asuna glanced briefly toward Siune and whispered, "If they start to draw again, cast Aqua Bind on them."

"All right. Oh my gosh, it's my first PvP fight in *ALO*. I'm so nervous."

To Asuna, it looked more like excitement than nerves in her eyes. She smirked, then turned back to the trio and took a few steps closer.

"If you weren't trying to PK us…then why were you hiding?"

The imp, who seemed to be the leader, glanced at his companions again, then answered: "We're waiting for a meet-up. We didn't want to get tagged by mobs while waiting for our friends, so we were hiding."

"…"

It was a likely answer, but somehow suspicious. Hiding spells had a considerable mana cost while active, so they would need to be drinking an expensive potion a few times a minute to keep it up. And if they were able to get all the way to the end of this labyrinth, they shouldn't need to go to such lengths to avoid monsters.

But she didn't seem likely to spot any other cracks in their story. If pressed to it, they could dispatch the trio via PK themselves, but causing trouble with a major guild would be nothing but headaches down the road.

Asuna swallowed her doubts and nodded. "All right. We're here to tackle the boss, but if you're not ready yet, I assume you don't mind if we go first."

"Yes, of course," the skinny imp answered immediately, to her surprise. She had expected them to use more obsequious flattery to interfere with their attempt at the boss. He waved his two companions back and retreated to the side of the massive doors.

"We'll be waiting for our friends here. So, um, good luck," he said with a faint smile, then motioned to the sylph with his chin. The sylph raised his hands and began to chant spell words with practiced ease.

Soon, a vortex of green air swirled up from the caster's feet, covering the three of them. Eventually the color flickered and faded, leaving nothing behind but the wall.

"..."

Asuna stared in the direction of their hiding place with a frown on her lips, but eventually shrugged and turned to Yuuki. She seemed to have found nothing wrong with that suspicious inter-action; her purple eyes glittered with expectation as she stared at Asuna.

"...At any rate, let's go ahead and test the waters as planned," Asuna said, and the other girl grinned and nodded.

"Yeah, it's finally time! Let's do our best, Asuna!"

"Let's not test the waters, but go in expecting to beat it on the first try," Jun cajoled, to which Asuna could only smile.

"Well, that's the ideal. But you don't have to waste the expen-sive items to heal. Just let Siune and me do our best to cast heal-ing spells. Agreed?"

"Yes, Sensei!" Jun chirped mischievously. She poked the visor of his helmet and looked to the other five in turn.

"If you die, don't return to town immediately. Stick around and watch the boss's attacks. If we get wiped, we'll all go back to Rom-bal's save point. Jun and Tecchi will stay at the front and guard, using taunt skills to pull aggro. Talken and Nori will attack from the wings, being careful not to draw too much attention. Yuuki will be a free attacker, preferably from behind the boss. Siune and I will be at the back providing support."

"Got it," Tecchi boomed for the rest of the group.

Once Siune was done re-upping the team's buff effects, the two front members proceeded forward. Tecchi, who had a tower shield held up in his left hand and his heavy mace in the right, turned back to Asuna when he reached the doors.

Asuna gave him a nod, and Jun used the hand not holding his greatsword to touch the door. He tensed and pushed.

The black, gleaming rock doors creaked in protest, then split, rumbling the entire corridor with the sound of thunder as they opened. The interior was pure darkness.

Almost instantly, two pale fires lit themselves just beyond the door. Two more started to the left and right. At brief intervals, countless flames popped into being to eventually form a circle. It was an effect that happened on every floor, a countdown of sorts that allowed the challengers time to prepare before the boss finally appeared.

The boss chamber was a perfect circle. The floor was polished black stone, and vast. On the wall in the back was a door that led to the staircase going up to the next floor.

"Let's go!" Asuna cried, and Jun and Tecchi burst into the room. The other five followed.

Everyone took their spots in formation and raised their weapons just as a rough-hewn mass of polygons began to pop into existence in the center of the chamber. The little black cubes combined into a humanoid form with bursting noises, forming edges and gaining information and profile before their eyes.

At the end, it exploded into little tiny shards, revealing the full extent of the boss.

It was a dark giant standing a good thirteen feet tall. Its burly, muscled trunk sprouted two heads and four arms, each holding a menacing, ugly bludgeon.

The giant took a step forward, sending an earthquake rumble through the room. The extra volume of its upper half was not matched by the lower half, and it tipped forward perilously, but the two heads were still held high over Asuna and the others.

Four glowing red eyes glared at the intruders. The giant let out a deep bellow. The two upper arms raised hammers the size of battering rams, and the lower arms slammed massive, anchor-ready chains against the ground.

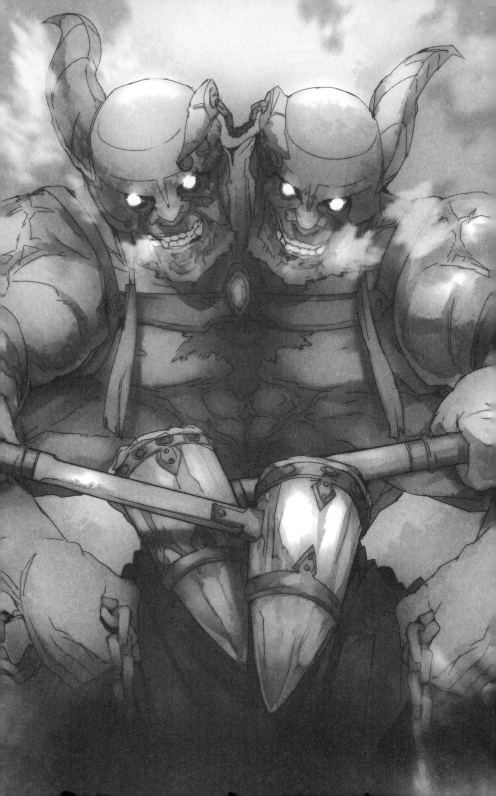

6

"Daaah, we lost!!"

Nori was the last to teleport, slapping Talken on the back as he gleefully lamented their defeat.

They were inside a domed building facing the central plaza of Rombal. The group had appeared around the save crystal set into a lowered depression in the middle of the room. They had, of course, been quickly crushed by the dark giant that was boss of the twenty-seventh floor.

"Darn, we tried so hard," Yuuki grumbled, until Asuna grabbed her by the collar. "Fwuh?"

The undine fencer dragged the imp girl off to the corner of the room. "Over here, everyone!"

Jun and the others followed, widemouthed with surprise. They had just been suggesting a return to the inn for a break and a rundown of their attempt.

There was no one else inside the dome, where the deceased respawned, but Asuna made sure they were gathered in a spot where their voices would not carry outside so she could address the group in privacy.

"We don't have time to hang around. Remember the three outside the boss chamber?" she asked quickly.

"Oh, yes," Siune said, nodding.

"Those were scouts from one of the major boss-beating guilds. They were watching for players outside of their guild attempting to challenge the boss. I'm guessing that on the floor before this, and the one before that, they were watching you go in just like that."

"I…I had no idea…"

"I'm guessing their intention isn't to interfere with your attempt, but to gain information for themselves. They see the attempts of small guilds like the Sleeping Knights as a test case to learn the boss's attack patterns and weak points. That way, they don't have to suffer the death penalty or potion cost themselves," Asuna explained.

Talken, the one with the round glasses, raised a hand, his fingers fully extended. "B-but, after we walked into the boss chamber, the door closed instantly. H-how could they have collected information if they couldn't even s-see our fight?"

"Well, this is my fault for not being careful…but toward the end, I noticed a little gray lizard slithering around Jun's feet. That's a Peeping spell—dark magic. It sends a familiar to track a target player and latch onto his or her sight to show the caster. It should have showed a debuff icon when the spell was cast on you, but only for a second…"

"Oh, dang. I never noticed it!" Jun exclaimed, looking guilty. Asuna patted him on the back.

"No, it's my fault for not warning you ahead of time. They must have slipped the spell onto you while Siune was rebuffing us just before we went inside. It would be really hard to notice a single momentary icon when there are a ton of them popping up."

"…Which could mean," Yuuki said, wide-eyed, clutching her hands to her chest, "it wasn't just a coincidence that the twenty-fifth- and twenty-sixth-floor bosses got beaten right after we tried them!"

There was surprise in her voice, but not a hint of anger or affront. Asuna felt a renewed sense of respect for the girl as she nodded. "I'm sure that was it. Because of your best efforts, all of the boss's information was laid bare for others to step in and utilize."

"Which would mean," Siune murmured, her shapely brows contracting, "that we've played the patsy role for them once again…?"

"…My God," Nori lamented, as the other five started to slump their shoulders, but before that, Asuna smacked Yuuki's armor.

"Nope, we don't know that for sure yet!"

"Huh…? What do you mean, Asuna?"

"It's two thirty in the real world right now, and it'll be hard to get a few dozen people together for a raid at this time, even for a big guild. At the earliest, it'll take them an hour—and we're going to strike before they can. Let's wrap up this meeting in five minutes, so we can be back at the boss chamber in thirty!"

"What?!" the mighty warriors all exclaimed in shock. Asuna glanced at the group and gave them a one-sided smirk she'd picked up from a certain someone.

"We can do this. We can beat this boss—even with our number."

"R-really?!" Yuuki blurted, leaning forward so hard that their noses nearly bumped.

"As long as we calmly and accurately hit its weaknesses. Here's the strategy: though the extra arms are tricky, the boss is a giant type, and the fact that it's not an abnormal creature type means that at least it has traditional facets we can exploit. We know it attacks by swinging down its hammers, lashing with its chains, and lowering its heads to charge. When its HP is half down, it adds a wide-range breath attack. When the HP goes farther down to red, it uses an eight-part Sword Skill with all four weapons…"

Asuna spread open a holo-panel on the floor, switched it to a text-entry window, and quickly typed up a list of the boss's attack patterns. Then she listed the specific defensive methods for each one.

"…So Jun and Tecchi, you can ignore the chains. Just focus on the hammers. Next is the weak points. Don't try to stop the hammer swings with your shields or weapons, just dodge them and let them hit the floor—that will cause a point-seven-second delay. Nori and Talken, make sure that you get major attacks in during that window. Also, its back has significant weaknesses. Yuuki, you stay on his rear at all times and use charge skills. Just watch out for the chains, as they go all the way around the back. Now, as for the breath attack…"

She hadn't talked this much at a strategy meeting since she was an officer in the Knights of the Blood, but Asuna didn't have time to reflect on the distant past. The other six nodded, listening intently.

A part of her noted that it was like being a schoolteacher. Asuna's lecture was done in four minutes. Next, she opened her inventory and materialized all the healing potions they'd bought with their preparation budget, as well as the parting gifts her friends had shared with them.

A pile of colorful glass bottles clattered across the floor. They distributed the potions in a ratio matching the damage each member had taken in their previous attempt. Then, they tossed the blue potions with mana recovery effects into Asuna's and Siune's pouches, completing the preparations.

Asuna stood up straight, looked at her new companions, and grinned. "I'll say it again. You…no, *we* can beat this boss. I've been fighting in this place for years, so take it from me."

Yuuki gave her usual dazzling smile and stated, "My hunch was right. I was correct to ask you for help—and that won't change, whether we succeed or fail. Thank you, Asuna."

The others all agreed. Siune, who seemed to be the second-in-command, said in a soft but clear voice, "Thank you very much. I am now certain that you were exactly the person we were hoping to find."

Asuna did her best to contain the sudden swell of emotion she felt within her. She held up a finger and winked.

"Let's hold all of that until we can celebrate. So…once again, let's do this!"

The group left Rombal again, flying for the labyrinth at maximum speed. They took the shortest, most direct route, which caught the attention of several monsters, but Nori's bewitching magic temporarily blinded them so the party could continue unmolested.

They reached the massive tower in just five minutes, flying straight into the entrance without stopping first, then racing the same route all the way up to the top. Of course, they couldn't just run through the middle of the monster groups unimpeded, but Yuuki took the reins and once again dispatched the enemy leaders.

Their timers read twenty-eight minutes when they reached the corridor that led to the boss chamber. The long, wide hallway curved left in a spiral as it headed toward the center of the tower.

"All right! Two minutes to go!" Jun shouted, and started a sprint for the goal in front of Yuuki.

"Hey! Wait, you!" she cried, racing after him with her hand outstretched.

At this rate, they might just be able to rub it into the bigger guild's face, Asuna thought as she ran along. The group plunged down the winding corridor until finally, the doors to the chamber came into view.

"…?!"

She sucked in a deep breath and put on the brakes when she saw what lay ahead. Yuuki's and Jun's boots scraped against the floor as they came to a stop.

"Wh…what is this?!" Jun murmured, next to Asuna.

The last seventy feet of the corridor to the boss chamber was jammed with a crowd of players, near twenty in all.

Their races were mixed, but there was one common feature: They all bore a single guild symbol on their color cursors. It was a shield with a horse in profile—the same thing as the three they'd caught waiting at the door.

We are too late?! They couldn't have gathered their members this quickly, Asuna thought ruefully. It wasn't enough people for a boss fight. Twenty people were three parties, less than half of the maximum raid size of seven parties of seven.

They were probably still waiting for the rest of their group to arrive. Making the very end of the labyrinth your meeting spot was a bold move, but that was probably a sign of how desperate they were.

This time, Yuuki finally looked somewhat upset. Asuna approached her and whispered into the girl's ear, hidden by long purple hair.

"Don't worry. It looks like we'll have time to try it once."

"…Really?" asked Yuuki, looking relieved. Asuna patted her shoulder and strode over to the group. Every one of them stared at her, but there was no surprise or doubt on their faces. In fact, there was an easiness that said they were enjoying the situation.

Asuna paid them no mind and marched right up to a gnome wearing particularly expensive-looking armor.

"I'm sorry, we'd like to fight the boss. Will you let us through?"

But the gnome, whose arms were folded forbiddingly, gave her the exact answer she was fearing: "Sorry, no passage."

"No passage…? What do you mean?" she asked, taken aback. The gnome's eyebrows bounced high as he shrugged.

"Our guild's going to fight the boss here. We're just making preparations now. You'll have to wait."

"Wait? How long?"

"About an hour."

Now Asuna understood their plan. Not only had they put those scouts there to watch for boss strategies, but they had more members ready to physically block the path in case any particularly able-looking parties happened to arrive while they were preparing.

She had heard rumors about certain high-level guilds monopolizing certain hunting areas, but she had no idea that they were brazenly claiming neutral ground regularly like this. This was the kind of tyrannical behavior that the army had engaged in, back in the old Aincrad.

Asuna did her best not to stifle her natural urge to blister. "We don't have time to wait around for that. If you're going to fight right away, that's one thing. But if you're not, we're going first."

"I'm afraid that's not happening," said the gnome, utterly unperturbed. "We lined up first. You'll have to wait your turn."

"In that case, come when you're actually ready. We can go in at any time, so it's not fair to make us wait a whole hour."

"Like I said, there's nothing I can do for you. It's orders from above, so if you've got a problem, you can take it up with Guild HQ back in Ygg City."

"But that'll take *us* an hour just to go back there!" Asuna finally yelled, her temper lost. She bit her lip and took a deep breath.

They weren't going to let the team pass, no matter how she negotiated. So what could they do?

What if she negotiated to give them all the items and yrd that the boss dropped, if they allowed the party to go in first? No, items weren't all the benefits of beating a boss. There was a huge pile of skill points to be gained, as well as the intangible honor of having one's name on the Monument of Swordsmen. These people would not bite.

If this were a different VRMMO, they might have the option of reporting unfair behavior to the GMs, but it was general *ALO* policy to have all players resolve differences on their own. GMs only got involved with system or personal account issues. Asuna was trapped.

The gnome glared down at her, sensing that their negotiation was over, and he turned to rejoin his fellows.

From behind Asuna, Yuuki called out to the gnome: "Hey, you."

He stopped and looked over his shoulder at the Absolute Sword's cheerful grin. "So you're saying that no matter how nicely we ask, you're not going to let us pass?"

"That's basically it, if you want to know."

He had been momentarily surprised by the frankness of Yuuki's question, but he regained his haughty attitude just as quickly. Yuuki kept her smile up as she said, "Oh. That's that, then. Let's fight."

"Wh-what?!"

"Huh?"

Asuna's confused shriek came at the same moment as the gnome's.

One of *ALO*'s more hardcore features was the ability to attack other players freely when in neutral territory. It was explained in the game's help menu that every player had the right to express his or her frustration with others through the use of a sword.

But actually attacking others had its own troubles beyond just what was stipulated in the rules—especially when your target was a member of a high-ranking guild. Winning that particular duel could mean receiving retribution from the guild at a later time, and you never knew when an in-game argument could spill out into the larger Net community. It was well known among those who weren't in the game explicitly for PKing that one should never pick a fight with a big guild.

"Y-Yuuki, you might not want..." Asuna started, pausing when she wasn't sure how best to explain all this. Yuuki just patted her on the back with a smile.

"There are some things you can't get across without confronting them, Asuna. Such as showing just how serious you are about something."

"Yep, she's right," Jun murmured from behind them. Asuna turned to see the other five members brandishing their weapons with calm acceptance.

"You guys..."

"They must be prepared for this possibility, too; they're the ones blocking the way. They'll be guarding this spot down to the last man, I expect," Yuuki said, throwing a glance at the lead gnome. "Isn't that right?"

"Uh...W-we're..." the man stammered, still surprised. The small imp girl drew her longsword and held the point out in midair. The smile vanished from her lips, and her eyes went hard and serious.

"Now draw your weapon," Yuuki commanded. As if possessed by her demand, the gnome pulled a large battle-ax from his belt and uneasily held it at the ready.

The next moment, the girl charged down the corridor like a gust of wind.

"*Nwuh...!*"

The gnome growled and grimaced, finally realizing what was happening. He swung his enormous ax, but it was far too late. Yuuki's obsidian sword came in low and bolted upward like a wave of darkness, catching him square in the chest.

"*Urgh!*"

That single blow was all it took for Yuuki to knock back the gnome, who vastly outweighed her. Next came a direct overhead slash. The sword bit into the gnome's shoulder with a heavy *thunk*, carving out a huge chunk of HP.

"Raaahh!!" he bellowed, truly enraged now, and swung his double-bladed ax down at Yuuki from the right. His speed was impressive and worthy of a party leader for a major guild, but the Absolute Sword calmly met the blow.

Kwing! A high-pitched metallic ringing diverted the ax just slightly, so that it passed inches over Yuuki's red headband. Normally, parrying was a trick that only worked on weapons in the same weight class or lower. The only reason her delicate, rapierlike sword could parry a tremendous battle-ax was the frightening speed with which she swung it. Such movement was not possible unless the avatar, the nervous system, and the Amu-Sphere that connected them were fused as one.

What kind of experience did one need to reach such heights? Asuna watched the battle with wonder and curiosity, as Yuuki's sword took on a pale blue glow. She was preparing a Sword Skill.

The gnome was already off balance from his failed heavy attack, and she caught him with four blows in the space of a breath: a strike to the head, a downward slash, an upward slash, and a full-power overhead slice. The glowing blue square left behind by the point of her sword burned in the gnome's body. It was the perpendicular four-part attack, Vertical Square.

"Gaaah!" the gnome roared, flying backward and crashing onto the floor. His HP bar dropped all the way to the red zone.

He himself must have hardly believed it, because his eyes darted to the upper right and went wide.

He looked back at Yuuki, and his expression of shock turned to rage. "You...you pulled a dirty sneak attack on me!" he snarled, rather inaccurately. When he got to his feet again, his twenty companions were switched into battle mode. The close-range fighters spread out to span the hallway, drawing their weapons.

Asuna automatically squeezed her World Tree wand, her mind ringing with the refrain of Yuuki's earlier statement.

There are some things you can't get across without confronting them, Asuna.

That wasn't just meant for this situation. It was a firmly held belief of the strange girl named Yuuki. She had been doing this all along, after all. She'd crossed blades with countless challengers in her street duels, coming into contact with their hearts in the process.

...I see...But of course...

Asuna found that she was smiling without realizing it. If you backed down from challenging other players because you were worried about retribution, there was no point in playing a VRMMO at all. The sword at her waist was not for show, nor was it a piece of precious jewelry. Not at all.

Asuna took a step forward, her boots clicking with intense purpose, drawing herself next to Yuuki. Jun and Siune took Asuna's right, while Tecchi, Nori, and Talken stood on Yuuki's left.

Something about their little party of seven caused the enemy force, three times their number, to falter a step back.

The tense moment was broken by a horde of footsteps, not from ahead, but from behind. The gnome looked over the Sleeping Knights' heads at the far end of the hallway and grinned with victorious smugness.

"...!"

Asuna turned back, dreading what she would see, as a huge number of color cursors appeared in her view. The guild tags were mostly new to her—an arrow on a crescent moon—but some of them contained the familiar horse on shield. That meant this was the other half of the raid party the gnome's people were waiting for. There ought to be nearly thirty of them, then.

No matter how tough Yuuki's team was, they couldn't beat seven times their number, especially when flanked on both sides. The foes outside of their weapon range alone would pick them off by magic or arrows.

This is my fault for waffling like that, Asuna thought, biting her lip with remorse. If she'd followed Yuuki's creed from the start, they might have blown through the twenty ahead of them and made it into the boss chamber.

But before she could apologize to her party, Yuuki brushed her hand. She could sense the girl's intent through her virtual skin.

I'm sorry, Asuna. My impatience got you dragged into this. But I don't regret a thing. That was the best smile I've seen from you since I met you.

The whisper seemed to sink directly into her head. Asuna squeezed back to impart her own message: *No, I'm sorry for being useless. Maybe this floor won't work out, but I'm sure we can defeat the next boss together.*

Their sentiments were sensed and shared by the other five. Everyone nodded and formed a rounded formation with a front and rear line. All thirty bearing down on them from the rear had apparently received a briefing about the situation, and were ready with their weapons drawn.

At this point, they just had to fight as long as they could. Asuna held her wand aloft, preparing an attack spell. A claw-wielding cait sith on the enemy's front rank flashed a carnivorous smile and snarled, "You don't know when to—"

But before he could finish his triumphant taunt, Asuna and every other player present in the corridor was brought to a halt by an even more unimaginable sight.

"Wh-what's that...?!" cried Nori, who was the first to notice it with her night vision. A second later, Asuna saw it as well.

From behind the approaching enemy reinforcements, who

were nearly twenty yards away now, something...some*one* was running sideways along the gently curving corridor wall. The silhouette was dark and hazy from the extreme speed.

Whoever it was, they were using the Wallrun skill that all of the more nimble fairy races could use: sylph, undine, cait sith, imp, and spriggan. But it normally only lasted a good thirty feet or so, while this figure had already traveled three times that length. It was a piece of acrobatics that was impossible without incredible dash speed.

But as soon as that thought registered in her mind—perhaps from the very moment she first saw the vague shadow—Asuna was certain she knew who it was.

The figure raced along the wall until it surpassed the reinforcement party and leaped off the wall to the floor, sparks spraying from the bottom of his boots as he slowed. He came to a stop in between the enemy and the Sleeping Knights, his back facing Asuna.

He sported tight-fitting black leather pants, a long black coat, close-cropped but layered black hair, and a particularly large one-handed longsword on his back.

This weapon was sheathed in a black hide scabbard imprinted with a white wyvern. That was the logo of Lisbeth Armory, a well-known shop along a main thoroughfare in Yggdrasil City. Asuna's best friend had crafted that splendid sword of a rare metal only found in Jotunheim.

The black-clad swordsman's hand blurred as it drew the pale blue longsword from his back and jammed it into the stone floor at his feet with a tremendous ringing. Thirty veteran fighters came to a screeching halt, shocked still by his force of presence.

Ironically, what he said next was extremely similar to what the ax-bearing gnome had just said to Asuna moments earlier:

"Sorry, this area is off-limits."

His voice was loud and clear but devoid of intensity. It was met with silence not just from the thirty reinforcements, but also the

twenty original guild members, as well as Asuna and the Sleeping Knights.

It was a slender salamander at the lead of the reinforcements who was the first to react to this cocky claim. He shook his head in disbelief, long auburn hair waving.

"Come now, Master Black. You don't honestly think that even you can take on this many people solo, do you?"

The swordsman, who had as many nicknames as there were ways to describe a person dressed all in black, shrugged his shoulders and said, "I don't know. I've never tried before."

The salamander, who appeared to be the leader of the guild alliance as a whole, snorted and raised his hand. "Of course you haven't. Well, let's see how you do…Mages, burn him."

He snapped his fingers. High-speed spell chanting emerged from the rear of the group. From their reaction speed to the clarity of their speech, they were well-trained sorcerers. Asuna's instincts were to start casting a heal spell, but the twenty members of the lead group behind them would not allow her that much time.

At that moment, the spriggan intruder turned at last.

The invincible grin that pulled up his left cheek was the same one she'd seen countless times through several different avatars. But the next moment, an eruption of spells from behind him turned his smile into a silhouette.

Yet Kirito the Black Swordsman did not show an ounce of consternation at the seven high-level attack spells hurtling toward him. It would have been pointless to dodge, after all—they were all single-target homing spells, and there was no escape in a corridor just sixteen feet across, where flight was prohibited to boot.

Instead, Kirito lifted the sword from the floor to rest on his shoulder, where it began to glow a deep crimson—the initiation of a Sword Skill.

The next moment, the corridor was filled with bursting color, a tremendous roar, and the shock of fifty-plus onlookers.

The seven-part skill that Kirito unleashed, Deadly Sins, neutralized—no, cut through—all of the oncoming attack spells.

"No...way..." Yuuki the Absolute Sword muttered. Asuna understood that feeling. But if you couldn't handle someone who did the impossible, the improbable, the implausible, then you couldn't handle the VRMMO player known as Kirito.

This was a non-system-defined skill that Kirito had developed, which he called "spell-blasting."

Long ago, during the old Aincrad, Kirito liked to use a special skill he called "arms-blasting," which was the accurate use of Sword Skills on weakened or fragile parts of his dueling opponent's weapon, in order to cause the item to break. It was an incredible piece of pure skill, requiring superhuman reaction speed and precision—but cutting through spells in *ALO* was even harder than that.

Attack spells almost universally had no physical form and resembled nothing more than a cluster of light effects. The only place they could be "hit" was at the exact center point of the spell. So a fast-moving spot the size of a pixel had to be hit with a Sword Skill, not a standard attack. Your ordinary physical weapon attack could not neutralize a magical attack. However, nearly all Sword Skills had some kind of elemental damage like earth, water, fire, and so on, which made them capable of colliding with magic. But because the system took control of the attack trajectory and speed when performing a Sword Skill, hitting the center of a spell was beyond difficult and into the realm of absolutely impossible.

In fact, Leafa, Klein, and Asuna had joined Kirito on his attempt to master the spell-blasting ability, and they had to call it quits after three days. Kirito claimed that the only reason he could pull it off was his conversion to *Gun Gale Online*, where he had lots of experience cutting bullets with a sword. "Every high-speed magic spell is slower than a bullet from a live-ammo rifle," he said with a straight face, which earned him three seconds of stunned silence from his friends.

For these reasons, Kirito was probably—no, unquestionably—the only player in Alfheim who could pull off this feat. And he only practiced it in secret, never in duels or with a party, so the members of this mammoth guild had never seen it done before.

"...What the hell...?" the long-haired salamander moaned, while his companions on either end of the corridor murmured similar sentiments.

"He cut the spells!"

"Sure it wasn't coincidence?"

"That's the thing..."

But true to their reputation as veteran players, the guild recovered quickly. At the salamander's orders, the front fighters drew their weapons, the roving fighters readied bows and polearms, and the rear guard resumed chanting spells. This time they weren't single-homing spells but multihoming and area-ballistic types.

Kirito turned back and gave Asuna another nod, then held up three fingers on his left hand. It wasn't a variation on the V-for-victory sign, of course, but a message that he would provide defense for three minutes. Even he didn't think that he could defeat thirty players on his own.

At last, Asuna understood why Kirito had shown up at this moment.

When he heard from her that she'd be assisting the Sleeping Knights in beating the floor boss, he already expected the big guild alliance would run interference. So he probably hid at the entrance to the tower, watching for alliance activity. When he saw more people enter the labyrinth than the Sleeping Knights could handle, he tossed aside his personal safety to buy them some time.

Three minutes. One hundred and eighty seconds. That amount of time passed in a blink at their forest cabin, but it was tremendously long in a PvP battle. She didn't doubt Kirito's ability, but could he really hold down so many players for such a long time? Should they send one of their seven to his aid...?

Two things cut through her moment's hesitation.

First, Kirito reached around his back with his left hand to grab the hilt of a second sword, which he drew loudly and clearly. It was a frighteningly elegant longsword with a deep golden blade. This was not a player-made weapon. It was the holy sword Excalibur, a legendary weapon sealed in the depths of the floating labyrinth in the underground realm of Jotunheim. They'd attempted the labyrinth with as many people as could fit on the back of Tonky, Leafa's flying monster friend, and were nearly wiped out entirely in the boss battle. But the sight of Kirito with his dual blades again gave him the aura of absolute dependability that made all that trouble worth it.

The reinforcements backed away slightly at the sheer force of presence the golden blade held. As if waiting for that instant of hesitation, a hardy bellow issued from behind the back row of enemies.

"Raaah! And I'm here, too, though I bet you can't see me!!"

The gruff, inelegant voice belonged to the familiar katana warrior Klein. Asuna rose on her tiptoes and saw an ugly bandanna and spiked red hair over the heads of the enemy. So Kirito wasn't the only one monitoring the labyrinth. But why did he show up so much later?

"You're late! What took you so long?" Kirito shouted from this side of the crowd. Klein yelped, "Sorry, I got lost!" from the other end. Asuna nearly wobbled and lost her balance.

Lastly, she noticed a small figure waving to her from Kirito's shoulder. It was their daughter, Yui, in her pixie form. The warmth of her adorable smile filled Asuna's heart.

Thank you, Yui. Thank you, Klein.

I love you, Kirito.

Asuna turned to Yuuki and whispered, "We can leave them to those two. Our job is to break through the twenty on the other side and make our way into the boss chamber."

"Okay, got it," Yuuki said crisply, after several high-speed blinks. She turned and held her longsword high, preparing an immediate Sword Skill. As her weapon began glowing purple, the others readied their weapons as well—Jun and Siune on the left wing and Tecchi, Nori, and Talken on the right.

The twenty members of the lead party and their gnome captain were confused at all of the rapid developments, but when they saw the Sleeping Knights start to go into action, they responded with admirable speed.

Once she heard the deafening roar of magic and Sword Skills clashing behind them, Asuna shouted, "Let's go!"

With Yuuki at the lead point, the seven formed a wedge and barreled forward. Likewise, the gnome's team roared and charged ahead.

The two sides clashed, resulting in a shock wave of consecutive light flashes. In an instant, the battle was plunged into chaos, and the sounds of fighting engulfed their end of the corridor as it had the other side.

Asuna knew from personal experience that Yuuki was a veteran dueler, but she was surprised to see that the other members still held their ground without an ounce of hesitation now that their foes had gone from monsters to humans.

Jun's two-handed ax and Tecchi's heavy mace made good use of their weight to crumble the enemy's formation, and Talken's long spear and Nori's quarterstaff snaked into the gaps that ensued. Meanwhile, Yuuki was making the best of her preternatural evasive ability to nimbly dodge the many strikes bearing down on her, then slip past the enemy's guard and counter with decisive slashes.

The Sleeping Knights fought with valiant skill against a group several times their number, but the enemy did not go down easily. The mages in the rear were casting continual healing spells to keep them going.

As was unavoidable in a massive, chaotic scrum like this, all the members aside from Yuuki steadily began to lose HP to incidental hits. Asuna and Siune began to cast healing spells as one.

Suddenly, two shadows slipped out of the group and sprinted

for them. They were assassin types, with light leather armor and nasty, glinting daggers in hand.

Upon realizing that they were, in fact, the same people who had been hiding in wait outside the boss chamber less than an hour earlier, Asuna instinctively changed her spell chant. She blazed through her specialty chant in just two seconds, and fine waterspouts rose from the sylphs' feet and tangled them, throwing the two to the ground.

She turned to Siune, who had just finished another healing spell, and whispered, "Can you manage the healing on your own?"

The slightly taller undine nodded at once. "Yes, I think I can hold us together."

"Then I'm going to go take out the enemy healers."

More than a minute had passed since the start of the battle, and the roar of battle behind them was fiercer than ever before. Kirito and Klein had to be throwing themselves into the midst of the enemy battalion to protect against magic attacks, but without a healer focusing on them, they had no way of making up that incidental damage. He'd said three minutes, but she wanted to wrap up this group in two to make it up to them. They needed to focus on winning quickly.

Asuna opened her window and hurled her wand into the inventory, equipping her beloved rapier instead. A band of silver light materialized around her waist, solidifying into a sword belt and scabbard of fine mithril.

She drew the long, slender weapon with a fine ringing and charged at the two sylphs who were still grappling with her Aqua Bind tangling spell. With a few merciless attacks at critical points, she quickly eliminated all of their HP.

Through the expanding cloud of their shattering remains, she peered at the close battle ahead. The churning sea of blades and attacks spanned the width of the corridor, but it seemed the right side was the thinner of the two.

Asuna took a deep breath and plunged forward, dashing at full speed with her rapier held low against her waist. Once she was up to a good momentum, she bellowed at full volume so Yuuki could hear her, facing the opposite direction.

"Yuuki! Dodge!"

"Huh…? Wha—?!"

Yuuki turned back and just leaped out of the way in time as she caught sight of Asuna's charge. Beyond her, the gnome leader was paused with his ax pulled back, and Asuna thrust her rapier forward, leaning as far over as she could go.

Numerous surges of white light leaped from the point, trailing around Asuna. Next, she felt her body begin to float. She was charging forward with such speed that the light trailed behind her like a comet.

"Whoaaa!!"

The gnome finally burst into motion, holding his two-handed ax sideways like a shield. But his attempt was just an instant too late, as the point of the rapier impacted the center of his body.

He flew high into the air, as if some enormous, rampaging beast had thrown him. Most of his HP had been carved away by Yuuki's sword already, and his body began to disintegrate and emit yellow light in midair.

Asuna the white-hot comet did not slow down after her first victim but continued in a straight line toward the enemy healers in the back. Three or four more foes met the same fate as their captain, some flying high and others collapsing to the ground. This was the strength of Flashing Penetrator, a long-range rapier Sword Skill that fell in both the "elite" and "charging" categories. It was nearly impossible to use in a one-on-one duel, owing to the considerable running start it required, but it was an extremely useful tool for breaking through enemy groups like this.

After piercing the wall of armor and shields and coasting for several more yards in the air, Asuna finally landed on the labyrinth floor. She screeched to a halt, her boots sending up sparks, and looked up with a knee to the ground. Four spell casters in robes and cassocks stared down at her in stunned silence.

Great. I have a feeling that "Berserk Healer" nickname is going to spread even further after this, Asuna thought ruefully as she pulled her rapier back.

In a group battle, it was not actually the ability of the close-combat fighters at the front that mattered but the ability of the backup forces in the rear. After Asuna eliminated all of the healing ability of the enemy's lead force, they didn't stand a chance against the Sleeping Knights with Siune's support.

Two minutes and eight seconds had passed.

She turned back to see Kirito and Klein, still locked in fierce battle with the reinforcements. The larger group was smaller than before, but the two men's HP levels, as indicated by their color cursors, were near the red zone.

Asuna felt a fresh wave of gratitude to the two men and the pixie on Kirito's shoulder, who was acting as their strategic radar. She turned back to the Sleeping Knights, all of whom were still alive, and shouted, "It's showtime! Let's beat this boss!!"

The other six responded in kind and hurtled forward. Asuna raced with all her speed for the dark, looming doors to the boss chamber.

Just as in their first attempt, Jun used his free hand to pry the way open. Beyond the heavy double doors burned two pale fires.

The slow tracing of the circle as the fires lit automatically was their grace period after opening the door, but the team had no need to wait for it now. The party of seven plunged deeper into the chamber. Asuna, who was the last inside, turned to her right and hit a stone button on the wall. This canceled the minute of extra time they had, instantly shutting the chamber doors.

The massive doors rumbled and began to close. Through the shrinking gap, they could see that the battle outside was entering its final phase.

The swordsman in black raised his right hand over a bloodred HP bar. At last, it was the two fingers that signaled victory to Asuna.

The boss chamber doors closed at last, shutting out all sound from the corridor. No one would be able to open them until the battle inside was finished.

Amid a heavy silence, the only action was the growing of the signal fires every two seconds. The line of flames was not even halfway around the circular arena. They had a good fifty seconds left until the boss appeared.

"Everyone, recover all your HP and MP with potions. Remember the strategy we discussed for the fight. The first few attacks are very simple, so stay calm and dodge them all," Asuna instructed. The other six nodded and took out little red and blue bottles.

When she realized they wanted to say something after recovering, Asuna looked at them expectantly. Yuuki took a step forward as the representative of the group and said, "Asuna...did those two men join in...to help us get through...?"

"...Yes," she replied, smiling. By now, Kirito and Klein would have lost their last HP and turned into little floating Remain Lights. In fact, knowing that nobody there would revive them, they probably just gave up and respawned at the save point.

Asuna gave the Sleeping Knights a stern look, realizing that they were probably preoccupied with the fate of the two men who had sacrificed themselves for their sake.

"Let's make it up to them by reporting that we successfully defeated the boss."

"...But this entire time, we've only gotten anywhere thanks to you and your friends, Asuna," Yuuki mumbled, biting her lip and hanging her head. Asuna patted her shoulders kindly. They had ten seconds until the boss. She needed to use that time to tell them something important.

"I've learned something very precious from you, too, Yuuki: There are some things you can't get across without confrontation."

Yuuki went wide-eyed with surprise, but Siune and the others instantly understood what Asuna was saying. Behind the smiling, nodding fairies, the final guiding flames burst into life, louder than the others.

"This is our last chance! While we're fighting in here, that guild's going to regroup and reunite in the hallway. We've got to hang in there so that when the doors open, all they see is our triumphant faces!"

When she was the vice commander of the Knights of the Blood, Asuna was often the one to deliver fiery speeches like this before a boss fight. But back then, her statements caused more tension in the ranks than morale boosting. She got them to clutch their swords but did not reach their hearts. Asuna was only thinking of effective strategic leadership and wasn't connecting with her emotions.

Hey...Yuuki. When this battle is over, tell me more about yourself. I want to know what worlds you've traveled, what adventures you've led.

She squeezed Yuuki's shoulders one last time, then took a step back. The rapier was in its sheath and stashed away, the tree-branch wand back in her hand and held high.

Where it pointed, a low, bass-heavy rumble heralded the arrival of angular, boulderlike polygons. The boss was materializing. The bulky, humanoid clump burst into countless shards, revealing a two-headed, four-armed giant.

"All right...Time for a rematch!"

Yuuki's clear voice, the shouts of the group, and the roar of the dark titan all overlapped.

7

Asuna flipped the cap off the bottle with her thumb, chugged the blue liquid inside, then checked the remaining amount.

Over the forty fierce minutes of battle, the waist pouch that had been stuffed with potions was now down to just three. The other healer, Siune, had to be at a similar point herself.

The attackers making up the front line were fighting as hard as anyone possibly could. They were successfully evading every one of the dark giant's attacks that were dodge-able. But both the wide-ranging poison breath that the creature's two mouths periodically emitted and the wild double-chain swings reached the entire battlefield and were extremely hard to counteract. Whenever either of them came into play, Asuna and Siune had to begin casting their most powerful heal spell, so they couldn't possibly get enough mana points.

Nori's staff, Talken's spear, and Yuuki's sword were all scoring countless clean hits, but something was wrong; it felt like they were striking an utterly impassable steel wall. The boss would sometimes cross its four arms in front of its body in a defensive stance, turning as hard as iron and deflecting all attacks, which only made the task more tiresome.

Asuna tried to swallow as much of her impatient frustration as she could with the mouthful of potion, and she strained to shout, as loud as possible, "We're almost there, guys! Almost there—we can do it!"

And yet, she had said the same thing five minutes earlier. The boss monsters in New Aincrad had no visible HP bars, so they could only estimate their success by the enemy's actions. The dark giant, which was slow and plodding at the start of the fight, was now raging in a berserk state, so it had to be getting to the end of its stamina, but that was still nothing more than an optimistic hope.

In a lengthy battle without a visible end, the backup rank only had to worry about the draining of their MP, but the forwards who were up close and personal with the enemy's furious attacks were draining their own willpower and concentration to fight. In a typical boss strategy, the tanks and damage dealers in the front line were supposed to switch out every five minutes at the most, according to orthodox theory. In that sense, the effort of the Sleeping Knights was extraordinary.

But their fatigue was impossible to ignore now. The only energetic response to her appeal came from Yuuki. Somehow, the little imp girl had managed to nimbly leap out of the way of the giant's hammers and chains, delivering steady damage with her sword, for dozens of minutes, without showing a single sign of exhaustion.

Until now, Asuna had believed that the source of Yuuki's strength was her unbelievable reaction speed, but now she had to consider a different answer. The strength of her mentality, her ability to keep swinging without losing concentration, might rival even Kirito's.

As she cast the umpteenth healing spell of the battle, Asuna compared the sight before her eyes to those in her distant memories.

On the seventy-fourth floor of the old Aincrad, Kirito had carried on a heroic solitary stand against a similar giant humanoid boss. He had evaded the enemy's furious onslaught with desperate parrying and leaping, his swords hurtling through the air with machine-gun speed, devastating the enemy's weak flanks with endless Sword Skill combos...

"Oh..."

An idea hit Asuna like a bolt of lightning. The resulting gasp caused her spell chant to fizzle out, producing a little puff of black smoke. She tensed in guilty surprise, but Siune's spell activated just in the nick of time. The HP bars of the fighters up front in the midst of a cloud of poison breath refilled to the safe zone.

When Siune looked over to see what had happened, Asuna held up her hand vertically in a sign of apology. "I just thought of something, Siune. Can you handle the healing for thirty seconds?"

"Yes, I'm fine. I've got mana to spare," replied Siune. Asuna motioned to her again, then raised her wand. She took a sharp breath and began to chant a different spell this time, as fast as she could manage.

As her spell words stacked up, glittering shards of ice appeared before her, coalescing into four sharp icicles. When the knives of ice were ready, a blue point of light appeared in the center of her vision: the aiming reticle of a nonhoming attack spell.

Asuna carefully moved her left hand, fine-tuning the location of the blue point, lining it up with the throats of the giant's two heads. As it stomped closer, it began to raise its two upper arms with their hammers for a massive strike.

"Yaah!!"

She swung her wand straight down. The four icicles flew forward, leaving pale blue trails behind them, striking true right into the necks of the two heads.

"*Guohhhh!!*"

The giant issued a tremendous scream, its hammer attack forgotten, and crossed its four arms in front to protect its body. It held that defensive position for five seconds, then raised its arms again, slamming the war hammers into the cobblestones.

An earthquake rumble ran through the floor, and Asuna had to focus hard on her feet to avoid losing her balance. "As I thought," she murmured.

Siune gave her a questioning look, so she explained. "I thought that defensive stance was a random effect, but it's not. The base of the neck is its weak point. I never gave it much thought, because I figured we wouldn't have time to search for it..."

"So we can beat it if we attack there?!"

"At the very least, it'll be more efficient...I think. But it's too high up."

The giant was a good thirteen feet tall, so even Talken's long spear was just short enough not to reach. Out in the open, they could fly up to attack it, but not inside the dungeon.

"We might need to use Sword Skills and expect a counterattack," Siune said. Asuna agreed. In order to extend airtime in nonflight areas, the only choices were charging Sword Skills or jumping first before starting a combination attack. Either option would end with a delay, which was likely to result in getting smashed as you fell defenseless to the ground. They could attempt resurrecting a dead player with spells, but the success rate wasn't perfect, and the casting time was exhaustingly long. In the meantime, they might fall behind on healing and end up dooming the entire party anyway.

But Yuuki would volunteer to do it without a second thought. Siune, who possessed an iron will at odds with her delicate undine features, nodded firmly.

"I'm going to go up and tell them the plan. Keep up the healing," Asuna said.

"Don't worry about it!"

Asuna pulled out two of her remaining potions, handed them to Siune, then raced to the front row. She covered the fifty feet in an instant, and as she approached the giant, a chain hurtled toward her from the side. She ducked her head to avoid it, but the sinker at the end caught her on the shoulder, taking HP with it.

Undeterred, she kept running until she was just behind the party leader. "Yuuki!!"

The imp girl turned around midswing, her eyes wide. "Asuna! What is it?!"

"Listen! It has a weak point. If you aim for the base of its necks, you can do major damage."

"Weak point?!" Yuuki turned back to the giant and stared at its heads. A hammer like a giant barrel came bearing down from above, so they had to dodge out of the way, then leap straight upward to avoid the shock wave through the floor.

Yuuki shouted, "It's too high...I can't jump up that far!"

"Good thing we've got the perfect stepping stone." Asuna grinned, glancing over at Tecchi, who was protecting Nori from the swinging chains with a shield the size of a door. Yuuki grinned back instantly, catching on.

They sprinted forward, swinging around about ten feet behind Tecchi. Yuuki put her free hand to her mouth and bellowed in a way that her tiny body was never meant to. "Tecchi! Next time he swings the hammers, duck down right away!!"

The large gnome turned back, his small eyes full of surprise, but he nodded his understanding. After the dark titan had finished swinging its chains, it pulled back its boulderlike torso to suck in a huge breath. It held it momentarily, then blew out a black gas from both mouths. They were surrounded by the stench of sulfur, and the HP of everyone in front began to drop.

But with perfect timing, as soon as the breath attack was over, blue light descended from above, healing their damage. The giant followed up by raising its hammers high overhead in its upper arms. Yuuki tensed, preparing to sprint. Asuna quickly called out to her. "This is our last chance! Good luck, Yuuki!"

Without turning back, Yuuki said, "I've got it, Big Sis!!"

Big...Sis?

Asuna blinked in surprise at the unexpected title, but the girl was already off and running. Up ahead, the giant slammed the hammers against the ground, strong enough to break through the earth. Heavy sound rattled around the room, and a circular shock wave spread out from the landing points. Tecchi crouched down to defend.

Then Yuuki leaped, her left foot landing on Tecchi's broad left shoulder, then her right on the top of his thick helmet.

"Uraaaah!!" she screamed, and leaped high into the air, so high that she might have had invisible wings. As she approached the giant's chest, she drew back the sword in her right hand.

"Yaaah!!" she shrieked again, thrusting forward with tremendous speed at the base of the two necks. The circular chamber was momentarily lit with blue and purple.

When a Sword Skill was activated in midair, the user would not fall to the ground until after the skill was entirely finished, even in nonflight areas like the labyrinth tower. Yuuki hovered before the black titan, her right hand flashing like lightning. Five thrusts from upper right to lower left. Another five in an intersecting line. With each jab of the sharp point to the enemy's critical spot, the giant's arms twitched, and it howled in pain.

Ten thrusts in the shape of an *X* finished, Yuuki twisted hard to the right, placing her left hand against the flat of her blade.

Asuna had to squint against the flash that erupted from the sword. It was as if Yuuki's obsidian sword had momentarily turned to diamond. The now pure-white sword plunged into the connecting point between the two necks, the very center of the *X*, with the ringing of a bell. The sword plunged all the way in to the very hilt.

The giant's scream halted, and it froze at an unnatural position. Asuna, Jun, Tecchi, and even Yuuki herself, with her arm outstretched, all sat motionless in the midst of a silent pause in time.

Eventually, around the sword's point of entry, myriad white cracks formed in the giant's black skin. The cracks gave way to the sheer pressure of the light from within, growing longer and thicker. They slowly engulfed the creature's torso and limbs.

With a sound like a dead, dry tree cracking, the dark titan split into two, right along the joint of the two necks. Like a glass sculpture being crushed under pressure, the thirteen-foot-tall body burst into pieces of all sizes. The blast of white light blew outward

with physical force, ruffling Asuna's hair. A mixture of deep bass and screaming treble bounced off the walls of the dome and eventually trailed away in a sound of hard metal.

The blue guide flames that lit the circular dome in eerie light shook briefly, then turned to the ordinary orange. Suddenly, the boss chamber was lit with bright, natural light, driving away the last remnants of spookiness.

With a heavy *clank*, the door on the far end, which led to the next floor, unlocked itself.

"...Ha-ha...We...did it..." Asuna rasped, falling to the floor. When she looked back at the spot where the boss had disappeared, she met the dazed gaze of Yuuki.

The small imp girl blinked quickly for several seconds, then a faint smile spread over her lips. Eventually it grew into a more familiar full smile, until it reached a level of radiance she had never before shown.

Yuuki rushed toward Asuna, thrusting her sword noisily back into its sheath. When she was still a good distance away, she leaped, arms wide, and crashed right into Asuna.

"Oof!" Asuna grunted theatrically and flopped onto the floor with Yuuki. After a brief moment of staring into each other's eyes at point-blank range, they shouted in unison.

"Aha-ha-ha...We did it...We won, Asuna!"

"Yeah, we did it! Aaah...I'm exhausted!!"

They fell back onto the floor, limbs splayed, Yuuki resting on top. Around them, their five companions got up from similar positions of fatigue and assumed bold victory poses, cheering raucously.

Suddenly, Asuna realized that she was hearing a heavy sound from the direction of her head. She craned her neck and saw, upside down, that the entrance doors were slowly opening. Countless silhouettes were crammed into the space.

It was, of course, the raid party that had attempted to block their way, plunging in through the doors with angry bellows. Their attitude and momentum slowed quickly when they recognized the bright orange light filling the chamber. They looked around in surprise.

The long-haired salamander at the very head of the fifty-man team met Asuna's gaze. His face evolved from shock to understanding to frustration, which brought a savage thrill to her heart.

"Heh-heh…"

Asuna, Yuuki, and the others all smirked, flashing the V-sign as they lay on the floor.

After the guild moved on—but not before several dozen warnings and parting remarks—Asuna and the Sleeping Knights opened the door in the back of the chamber. They climbed the spiral staircase and emerged from a little pavilion into the unexplored twenty-eighth floor. They flew straight to the nearby city, where Yuuki activated the portal gate in the town square, thus completing the boss quest.

They used the glowing blue gate to immediately return to Rombal, where they formed a circle in a nook of the plaza and exchanged high fives.

"Good job, everyone! It's finally over!" Asuna said with a smile, but she felt a pang of sadness. As a simple hired sword, the completion of their quest meant a farewell was coming.

But no, they could still be friends. There was plenty of time for that, she considered. At that moment, Siune clapped her on the shoulder. Her delicate features were deadly serious.

"No, Asuna. It's not over yet."

"…Huh?"

"Something very important is still left."

The look on her face reminded Asuna about the Monument of Swordsmen in Blackiron Palace. That was right—their goal wasn't explicitly to beat the boss, but to leave all of their names on the monument, as proof of their guild's existence. It was too early to celebrate, then.

But Asuna was not expecting Siune to say, "We need to have a party."

Her knees buckled and she shook a fist in mock outrage, then set her hands against her waist. "Yes, you're right! We need to celebrate."

Jun smirked and said, "After all, we've got the budget for it now! Where will we hold it? Should we rent out a fancy restaurant in some big city?"

"Oh..."

Asuna looked at the rest of the group, steepling her fingers with a sudden idea. She'd only known these people for two days, but she was absolutely certain that her old friends would get along with them just fine.

"Well, if that's what we're going to do...why don't you come to my player home instead? It's a bit small, though."

Yuuki's face suddenly burst into sunshine. But for some reason, her smile melted away like snow under heat. She bit her lip and hung her head.

"Um...Yuuki? What's wrong?" Asuna asked, surprised. But the normally cheerful girl would not raise her head. Siune spoke for her instead.

"...Well...I'm sorry, Asuna. I hope you won't take offense, but...you see, we..."

But she never finished that sentence. Yuuki sucked in a sharp breath, face still downcast, and grabbed Siune's hand. The girl's lips were shut tight, and there was a painful look in her eyes as she stared at the older woman. Her lips twitched a few times, ready to say something, but no sound emerged.

Siune seemed to understand what she meant, however. A faint smile played over her lips. She patted Yuuki on the head and turned to Asuna. "Thank you, Asuna. We will honor your invitation and pay a visit."

Asuna gave them a quizzical look, uncertain of what their little exchange meant. However, Nori scattered the odd atmosphere with a hearty cheer. "First thing we gotta buy is booze! A whole barrel of it!"

"You won't find your favorite distilled sweet potato liquor here, Nori," Talken interjected, pushing up his glasses.

She hurled fierce insults at his back: "Say what? When did I ever say I liked that stuff? The only thing I drink is finely aged *awamori* from Okinawa!"

"In terms of their lack of charm, they're basically the same thing," Jun interrupted, prompting laughs from the group. Asuna joined in the laughter, glancing at Yuuki again. A smile was sneaking back onto the girl's face, but the hint of sadness lingered in her eyes.

They ventured into Rombal's central market and bought a feast's worth of alcohol and food, then teleported to the twenty-second floor. Asuna led the way, taking off from the little village and heading south over the snow-piled forest. When they had crossed an iced-over lake, a little clearing containing a small log cabin came into view.

"D-down there?!" Yuuki marveled.

Asuna nodded. "Yep, that's it…Oh!"

No sooner were the words out of Asuna's mouth than Yuuki sped up, her arms wide. She dropped straight toward the front garden of the cabin, sending up a huge cloud of snow, as well as a flock of startled birds from the nearby trees.

"…Good grief."

Asuna laughed as she shared a look with Siune, then spread her wings for a soft landing. She glided down and landed out front, where Yuuki grabbed her arm and impatiently pulled her in the direction of the door.

If any of their friends were already home, she would have introduced them all, but the cabin was empty. It made sense that Kirito and Klein wouldn't be back yet from the save point after helping them in the labyrinth, but the absence of Liz and the other girls was perhaps a sign that they anticipated this possibility and left them a peaceful place for the little team to celebrate in privacy.

"Oooh, ahhh! So this is your home!" Yuuki bubbled, examining the table growing from the floor, the burning red furnace, and the swords hung on the wall. The other six gathered around the table and opened their inventories to remove the food for the feast. Soon there was a pile of mysterious drinks and snacks on the table.

They opened up the wine—in a barrel, at Nori's request—and poured the golden liquid into glasses, completing the preparations. Jun grabbed Yuuki to stop her from admiring Asuna's spice collection in the kitchen and pulled her out to the living room table.

Tasked with leading the toast, Yuuki held her glass high with a radiant smile. "So, to celebrate conquering the boss...Cheers!"

With a group chorus and the clinking of glasses, everyone proceeded to drink. In no time, the party was fully underway.

As Jun and Tecchi excitedly discussed the boss they'd just beaten and Nori and Talken got to talking about the various types of alcohol in *ALO*, Yuuki and Siune told Asuna about the VRMMO worlds the Sleeping Knights converted from.

"The absolute worst one, without a doubt, was an American game called Insectisite," Yuuki said with a grimace, squeezing her body with both arms.

"Oh, yes...that one." Siune grinned sourly.

"So...what was that one like?"

"Bugs! Bugs everywhere! Of course, the monsters are bugs, but so are the players! At least I was an ant that walked on two legs, but poor Siune—"

"No! Don't say it!"

"—was a giant caterpillar! She'd shoot silk out of her mouth..."

At that point, Yuuki dissolved into laughter. Siune pouted, and Asuna couldn't help but join the giggles.

"That's great. So you've been traveling all over different worlds..."

"What about you, Asuna? You seem like you have a long VRMMO history."

"I've been, umm, only here. It took a long time to save up the money to buy this house, you know..."

"I see."

Yuuki looked up and examined the living room, her eyes narrowed. "It's really a lovely place, this house. It reminds me...of the old days."

"Yes, exactly. I feel very comfortable and relieved when I'm here."

Siune was nodding as well, but then she gasped faintly, as if remembering something.

"Wh-what is it, Siune?"

"Oh no, I forgot! Speaking of money...when we made our deal for Asuna's help, we said that we'd give her everything the boss dropped. And then we went and spent all that money on this stuff."

"Oh, man! I totally forgot, too!"

Asuna laughed and waved her hand to indicate to the upset Sleeping Knights that it was no big deal. "It's just fine. As long as I get something, that's all I— Actually, no," she finished, taking a deep breath.

She realized that it was her chance to finally say something she'd been thinking about since before the boss fight. Asuna put on a serious look. "I don't need anything after all. Instead, I have a request."

"Huh...?"

"Listen...I know that our contract ends here. But...I want more time to talk to you, Yuuki. There are still so many things I want to ask."

Asuna wanted to know how she could be as strong as Yuuki was. She continued. "Will you let me join the Sleeping Knights?"

She hadn't joined a guild since being reborn as a fairy in *ALO*. There had been invitations, of course, and they'd discussed making their own small guild with Kirito, Liz, and the others, but they'd never gone ahead with it.

It had to be because there was still a lingering sense of

fear about guilds. For more than a year, Asuna had been the subleader of the guild that was considered the strongest in the game. The guild demanded ironclad order and a steel will from its members, and she upheld that attitude by never smiling at others. Back then, she was feared but never revered. And she was afraid that if she joined a guild in *ALO*, it would send her back into that mindset.

But today, Asuna was completely at home among the Sleeping Knights and felt no consternation whatsoever about making orders. That was because Yuuki and the others had easily, comfortably eclipsed the barriers Asuna erected around her heart. The time she spent with them could only lower those walls. It would teach her true strength. Asuna herself didn't realize she possessed that desire, but Kirito and Klein had given her support through action, not words. They hadn't looked upset when she mentioned working with another guild; they had been perfectly supportive.

Yuuki didn't respond at once to Asuna's request. She bit her lip. Her big, wide eyes wavered with indecision again.

Suddenly, Siune and the four others were silently watching Asuna and Yuuki as well. For a long, long moment, Yuuki stared at Asuna without a word. When her quavering lips opened at last, her voice shook.

"Um...um, Asuna, listen. We...the Sleeping Knights...are going to break up soon...probably by the spring. After that, we won't really be able to play much of the game..."

"Yeah, I know. Just until then. I...I want to be friends with you guys. We have enough time for that...right?" Asuna asked, leaning forward and looking into Yuuki's purple eyes. But, for perhaps the first time ever, Yuuki averted her gaze. She shook her head.

"Sorry...I'm sorry, Asuna. I'm...really sorry."

There was such open pain in Yuuki's repeated apology that Asuna couldn't push her any further.

"Oh...okay. No, I'm sorry for pressing you like that, Yuuki."

"Um...Asuna, I...we..." Siune started, trying to fill in for Yuuki, but surprisingly, she was having trouble finding the right words as well. Asuna noticed that the rest of the group had similarly pained expressions, and she clapped her hands together in an attempt to fix the gloomy mood.

"Sorry about getting weird on you guys. Let's fix the mood by going to see the thing!"

"What thing...?" Siune asked. Asuna patted her and the downcast Yuuki on the shoulder.

"You're forgetting something very important! I'm sure that by now, they've updated the Monument of Swordsmen down in the palace!"

"Oh, right!" Jun erupted, getting to his feet. "Let's go! We can take a picture!!"

"Yeah! Shall we?" Asuna asked again. Yuuki finally raised her head and smiled weakly.

Asuna surveyed the central plaza of the Town of Beginnings for the first time in ages, dragging the still-lethargic Yuuki by the hand.

"Gosh, this place is so big...All right everyone, this way!"

She wove her way through the flower beds until the rectangular Blackiron Palace came into view ahead. It was one of the most famous tourist destinations in Aincrad, so there were newbies and veterans alike milling about the castle.

They headed through the main gate and into the imposing building, the interior air chilly on the skin. The sound of boots clicking on the steel floor echoed endlessly off the unfathomably high ceiling.

Asuna and the Sleeping Knights headed toward the great hall in the back, adding to the din. They had to pass through two doors before they emerged in a space that was relatively peaceful. A huge, lengthy monument of iron sat in the center of the room.

"There it is!"

Jun and Nori ran past Asuna and Yuuki. They arrived at the

foot of the Monument of Swordsmen a few seconds later. Asuna looked for the end of the sprawling list of names contained on the monument.

"Oh...there they are," Yuuki muttered. Her hand suddenly clenched in Asuna's, and the fencer spotted it as well. Almost at the very center of the gleaming black monument, there was an entry reading HEROES OF THE 27TH FLOOR, below which there were seven names.

"There they are...There are our names..." Yuuki repeated in a daze. Asuna noticed that the girl's eyes were moist, and she felt a lump in her own throat.

"Hey, time to take a picture!" said Jun from behind them.

Asuna grabbed Yuuki's shoulder and spun her around. "C'mon, Yuuki. Smile," she said.

That finally got Yuuki to crack a grin. With the others lined up in front of the monument, Jun used the pop-up menu of a Screenshot Crystal to set a timer, then let go. The crystal hung in place in the air, a countdown running over it.

He trotted over and squeezed between Yuuki and Tecchi. They all smiled, and the crystal flashed with a shutter sound.

"Okay!" Jun said, rushing back to check, as Asuna and Yuuki turned to look at the Monument of Swordsmen again.

"We did it, Yuuki," Asuna said, patting her on the head. Yuuki nodded and stared at the seven names for a long time.

Eventually, she mumbled, "Yeah...I finally did it, Big Sis."

"Hee-hee!" Asuna couldn't contain her giggle in time. "You did it again, Yuuki."

"Huh...?" Yuuki looked back at her in complete bewilderment.

"You called me 'Big Sis,' remember? Back at the boss chamber. I mean, it's very cute and flattering, but—?!"

Asuna stopped in midsentence. She hadn't meant anything serious by it.

But Yuuki was covering her mouth with a hand, her eyes wide. The purple irises filled with clear drops momentarily, dripping down her cheeks.

"Y…Yuuki?!"

Asuna tried to reach out to the girl, but Yuuki took a few steps backward. Her lips opened, uttering a hoarse croak. "Asuna… I, I—"

Suddenly, she turned away, wiping at her tears and waving her left hand. That brought up her menu window, which she touched with trembling fingers. Her small body was engulfed in a pillar of white light.

And just like that, Yuuki the Absolute Sword, invincible warrior, disappeared from Aincrad.

8

Asuna looked down at the piece of paper in her hand to ensure that the string of letters written on it indeed matched the title on the side of the large building.

She was in the Tsuzuki ward of Yokohama. The building sat nestled between hills rich with greenery. Given its fairly low height, the design surrounded by plants and trees, and the rolling hills, it didn't seem like they were in a big city at all. But in fact, it was less than thirty minutes away from Asuna's home in Setagaya, using the Tokyu Line.

The building was still new, and the brown tiles on the exterior gleamed in the low winter sun. It struck Asuna as similar to the place where she had slept for so long. She put the piece of paper back in her pocket.

"Are you in there, Yuuki?" she muttered. She wanted to see the girl, but she also hoped that she wasn't in there.

After a brief period of uncertainty, Asuna straightened up the lapels of the coat she was wearing over her uniform, and she started walking toward the front entrance.

Three days had passed since Yuuki the Absolute Sword disappeared from Aincrad.

When Asuna closed her eyes, she could still see her tears, just before she logged out at the Monument of Swordsmen. She didn't think she would ever forget them, even if she tried. She needed to see her again so they could talk. But all the in-game messages she sent received a stock "this user is not logged in" response, and they hadn't been opened yet.

She figured that the other Sleeping Knights would know where Yuuki was, but when she visited their favorite hangout place, the inn in Rombal, only Siune was there. She had looked down and shaken her head.

"We haven't been able to contact Yuuki since then, either. She hasn't been full-diving at all, much less playing *ALO*, and we hardly know anything about her real-life details. Plus…"

Siune stopped there. She gave Asuna a somewhat anxious look. "Asuna, I don't think that Yuuki wants to see you again. Not for her sake, but for yours."

Asuna was stunned into silence. She finally found her voice a few seconds later.

"Wh…why? I mean…I could tell that Yuuki and the rest of you were trying hard not to get too close to me. If I'm just bothering you, I'll leave her alone. But…I don't understand what you mean by saying it's for my sake."

"It's not bothering!" Siune said vehemently, her perpetually serene attitude broken for this one instant as she shook her head. "We truly are very happy to have found you. The fact that we were able to create such wonderful memories here at the end is thanks to you, Asuna. We cannot thank you enough for your help with the boss and your desire to join our guild. I'm sure Yuuki agrees with me there. But…please, I beg of you, just forget about us now."

She waved her hand to call up a window. A trade prompt appeared in front of Asuna.

"It's a bit earlier than we expected, but the Sleeping Knights should be breaking up soon. I am putting together our payment to you here. It is the loot the boss dropped, as well as all of our items..."

"I...I don't want it. I can't take them," Asuna said, smacking the CANCEL button. She stepped closer to Siune. "Is this really good-bye? I...I like you, and Yuuki, and everyone else. I thought that even if the guild broke up, I could still be friends with all of you. Or was that just me...?"

The old Asuna would never have said such things. But in just the few days that she'd been working with Yuuki's party, she could feel herself changing. And that just made their imminent farewell that much worse.

Siune looked down and shook her head. "I'm sorry...I'm sorry. But it's for the best if we say good-bye here...I'm sorry, Asuna."

And she, too, opened her window and logged out to escape the scene. After that, it wasn't just Yuuki; Siune, Jun, Nori, and the others did not log in to *ALO* at all.

It had only been a few days together. Asuna had assumed they were friends, but maybe she was wrong about that. But the Sleeping Knights left a deep, unshakeable impression on Asuna's heart. She knew she could never forget them.

The third term at school had already begun, but even seeing Kazuto (Kirito), Rika (Lisbeth), and Keiko (Silica) in real life for the first time in weeks did not bring Asuna cheer. Behind her eyelids and deep in her ears, she saw and heard Yuuki. "Big Sis," she had called Asuna. And when she realized that she had done it, she cried. Asuna wanted to know why.

And then Asuna got a text message from Kazuto yesterday, saying he would be waiting for her on the school roof at lunch.

There were no other students on the roof of the concrete building, exposed to the chill northern wind. Kazuto was leaning on a thick air circulation pipe as he waited for Asuna.

In real life, he didn't seem to be gaining any weight, even though it had been more than a year since he was released from

SAO. His sister, Suguha, was making sure he ate properly, so there was no concern about his nutrition, but either he was working off all the calories with jogging or the gym, or his frenetic virtual battles were somehow burning off his physical energy.

He had his hands in his pockets, top jacket button open, and long bangs waving in the wind, an appearance that was the same as in the old Aincrad days, just with a different outfit and height. Asuna rushed over to him and bumped her forehead right into the cradle of his shoulder as he looked up.

She wanted to express all of the churning emotions that tortured her gut, but Asuna couldn't even put what she was feeling into words. She squeezed her eyelids shut, trying to stifle the oncoming sobs. Kazuto gently patted her back. He murmured into her ear, "Do you still want to see the Absolute Sword?"

That simple question encompassed all of Asuna's desires. He was right: She wanted to see Yuuki again; she believed in her heart that Yuuki wanted the same thing.

Asuna nodded, and Kazuto continued. "She told you that you shouldn't see her again, didn't she? And you still want to?"

She had already told him all about the results of the twenty-seventh-floor boss battle, their unexpected parting afterward, and Siune's final comments, so Kazuto's questions were coming after he had formulated his own thoughts about the matter.

Asuna nodded again. "Yes, even still. I just want to see Yuuki and talk to her again. I have to do it."

"I see," Kazuto replied. He put his hands on her shoulders to put space between them, then pulled a small piece of paper out of his jacket pocket. "If you go here, you might be able to meet her."

"Huh...?"

"It's just a possibility, nothing more. But...I happen to believe that she's there."

"H...how do you know that...?" Asuna asked in a daze, taking the folded scrap of paper.

Kazuto looked up at the sky. "Because that's the only place in Japan where they're holding a Medicuboid clinical study."

"Medi...cuboid?" Asuna asked, turning the unfamiliar term over in her head. She opened the scrap of paper.

Inside, it read: *Yokohama Kohoku General Hospital*, along with an address.

Asuna passed through the pristinely clean double set of automatic doors and into the amply lit entrance, where she was greeted by the familiar scent of disinfectant.

She passed through the lobby full of mothers with small children and elderly patients in electric wheelchairs on her way to the reception desk.

On the form next to the window, she entered her name and address, but stopped at the spot asking for the name of the patient she wanted to visit. All Asuna knew was the name "Yuuki," and she didn't even know if that was the girl's real name. Kazuto had said that even if she was there, there was no guarantee Asuna could confirm that or be able to see her. But after coming this far, she couldn't possibly give up. She steeled her courage and took the sheet to the counter.

A nurse in a white uniform was on her computer terminal on the other side of the desk. She looked up as Asuna approached. "Are you here for a visit?" she asked, smiling.

Asuna nodded awkwardly. She handed over the form, still incomplete, and said, "Um...I want to meet someone, but I don't know her name."

"Pardon?" the nurse asked, her eyebrows drawn together in suspicion.

"I think it's a girl around age fifteen, and her first name might be 'Yuuki,' but it also might not."

"We have very many inpatients here, so I'm afraid that's not enough to narrow it down."

"Um...I believe she might be here undergoing a Medicuboid test."

"Patient privacy rights means that we can't..."

Further back behind the counter, an older nurse looked up and stared at Asuna. She leaned over and whispered something into the ear of the nurse who was providing reception.

The original blinked in surprise and turned back to Asuna. In a more formal tone, she awkwardly asked, "Pardon me, but what is your name?"

"Uh, er, my name is Asuna Yuuki."

She slid the form over the desk. The nurse took the sheet, glanced at it, and handed it to her coworker.

"May I see some form of identification?"

"O-of course."

She pulled her wallet out of her coat pocket and extracted her student ID. The nurse closely compared the photo on the card to Asuna's face, then nodded with satisfaction and asked her to wait while she picked up the nearby phone.

After a few short comments on the internal line, she told Asuna, "Dr. Kurahashi will see you in Internal Medicine Two. Go to the fourth floor in the front elevator, then proceed to the right and give this to the receptionist there."

The tray she held out contained Asuna's ID and a silver pass card. Asuna picked them up and bowed.

She ended up waiting at the fourth-floor reception bench for nearly ten minutes before she noticed someone in white rushing over to her.

"Hi! I'm sorry, forgive me. My apologies for the wait," said the small, plump doctor, who looked to be in his early thirties. His hair was parted to the side over his gleaming forehead, and he wore thick-rimmed glasses.

Asuna quickly got to her feet and bowed deeply. "N-not at all! I'm sorry to just show up out of the blue like this. I can wait as long as you need me to."

"No, it's perfectly all right. I'm off duty this afternoon. So you are, um, Asuna Yuuki, yes?" he said, his drooping eyes narrowing slightly as he smiled.

"Yes, that's me."

"Well, my name is Kurahashi. I'm Miss Konno's physician. I'm glad you've come to visit."

"Miss...Konno?"

"Ah. Her full name is Yuuki Konno. 'Yuuki' is written with the characters for 'cotton' and 'season.' I usually just call her Yuuki... She's been talking all about you every day, Miss Asuna. Oh, forgive me for being forward. I'm just used to hearing your name."

"No, Asuna is fine," she reassured him, beaming.

Dr. Kurahashi smiled shyly and pointed toward the elevator. "Why don't we go visit the lounge up above, rather than stand around here?"

They ended up sitting across from each other in the back of a wide-open waiting room. There was a nice view of the spacious hospital lot and the verdant area surrounding it through the large glass window. There were few people around, so the only disturbance to the room's air was the gentle humming of the air-conditioning.

Asuna wasn't sure which of the many questions she ought to ask first. Instead, it was Dr. Kurahashi who broke the silence.

"I understand you met Yuuki in a VR world, Asuna? Did she tell you about this hospital?"

"Er, no...She didn't, actually..."

"Ahh. I'm surprised you found us, then. In fact, Yuuki said that someone named Asuna Yuuki might be coming to visit her and to let the front desk know, so we were surprised to learn that she hadn't told you. I figured you wouldn't be able to find the place, so when they just called from downstairs a few minutes ago, it was quite a shock to me."

"Um...did Yuuki tell you much about me?" Asuna asked, to which the doctor nodded eagerly.

"Oh, indeed. The last few days, she hasn't spoken about anything else during my visits. However, every time she spoke to me about you, she always cried at the end. She's never been the type to cry about her own issues."

"But...wh-why...?"

"She wanted to be better friends, but she couldn't; she wanted to see you, but she couldn't. I'll admit, I can understand that feeling..."

For the first time, Dr. Kurahashi's face was pained. Asuna took a deep breath and summoned her courage to ask, "Yuuki and her friends said the same thing to me in the VR world before we broke apart. Why is that? Why *can't* she see me?"

She leaned forward, trying to avoid thinking about the steadily growing suspicion inside of her ever since she saw the word *hospital* on the note. Dr. Kurahashi looked down at his hands atop the table. Eventually, he said quietly, "To explain that, I need to start with the Medicuboid first. You are an AmuSphere user, I assume?"

"Er...yes, that's right."

The young doctor nodded and looked up. To her surprise, he said, "While it might not be fair to say this to you, it pains me to no end that full-dive technology was developed solely for entertainment purposes."

"Huh...?"

"The government ought to have put in the money and developed that tech for medical research. We would be a full year or two ahead of where we are now."

This direction of the conversation took Asuna by surprise. The doctor held up a finger and continued. "Just think about it. Imagine how useful the AmuSphere could be in a medical context. To people who are sight- or hearing-impaired, that machine is a gift from God. Unfortunately, those with hereditary brain damage are excluded, but consider anyone with nerve damage between the eyes and the nervous system. With the AmuSphere, that information goes straight to the processing center instead. The same applies to hearing. People who have lived their lives without the concept of light or sound can now experience the world the way it should be experienced, just by using that machine."

Asuna nodded at Dr. Kurahashi's impassioned explanation.

The use of the AmuSphere in this field wasn't a recent development. Once the headgear was made even smaller and had its own special lenses, the blind and deaf would be able to function exactly as everyone else in society.

"And it's not just signal reception that it can help with. The AmuSphere can also cancel bodily signals," he said, tapping the base of his neck. "By sending an electric pulse here, you can temporarily paralyze the nerves, producing the same effect as full-body anesthesia. So using an AmuSphere during an operation can also remove the remote chance of something going wrong with the anesthetic."

Asuna was surprised to find herself engrossed in the doctor's stories. But something occurred to her. Careful to mind her words around the medical expert, she timidly said, "But… isn't that impossible? The AmuSphere's interrupting signals are intentionally limited. I don't think an AmuSphere—or even the original NerveGear—could block out the pain of a doctor's scalpel…And even if you canceled out the spinal column signals, the nerves are still alive, so they'd react, right…?"

"Y-yes…that's true," Dr. Kurahashi said, startled at her knowledge. He recovered quickly and nodded several times. "No, that's absolutely true. The AmuSphere has low pulse output and a power-saving CPU, so there's a sharp limit on its processing power. It's fine for making a full dive into a Virtual Reality space, but the specs aren't up to the level necessary to provide Augmented Reality with the combination of a lens and the physical world. So for the moment, the biggest rush in government development is for the Medicuboid: the world's first medical-use full-dive device."

"Medi…cuboid," Asuna said, rolling the word on her tongue. She recognized that it had to be a combination of *medical* and *cuboid*.

The doctor grinned and continued. "It's still just a codename. Essentially, it boosts the AmuSphere's output, multiplies the density of the pulse-generating nodes, and increases processing speed. This is embedded into the bed so that it can cover the entire spine and not just the brain. It looks just like a white box... but if they can be built practically and put into use at hospitals all over, it will have a dramatic effect on medicine. Anesthesia will be unnecessary in nearly all operations, and we might even be able to communicate with patients suffering from locked-in syndrome."

"Locked-in...?"

"It's also known as a pseudocoma. The conscious, thinking parts of the brain are intact and functioning, but there's something wrong with the parts that control the body, so they cannot express their own will. The Medicuboid can connect to the deepest parts of the brain, so even someone in a state of paralysis might be able to rejoin society through the use of VR."

"I see...so this really is a 'machine of dreams' in the truest sense... even more than the AmuSphere built for playing games," Asuna murmured. But although Dr. Kurahashi had just been speaking of lofty dreams, this comment seemed to bring him back to reality. He looked downcast, removed his glasses, and sighed heavily.

With a little shake of his head, he smiled sadly. "Yes, that's it. A machine of dreams. But...machines have a limit, of course. One of the areas in which the Medicuboid is most highly anticipated is...terminal care."

"Terminal care..." Asuna repeated, unfamiliar with the English term.

"It's also known as hospice care," the doctor explained softly. Asuna felt as though she'd been doused with freezing water. She gaped, her eyes wide. Dr. Kurahashi put his glasses back on with a kindly smile. "Later on, you might wish that you had stopped listening here. No one will criticize you for making that choice now. Yuuki and her friends really are thinking of you when they said this."

But Asuna didn't hesitate. She was ready to face whatever reality had in store, and she felt she had a duty to do it. She looked up and said, "No...please continue. This is why I came here."

"I see," Dr. Kurahashi said, smiling again and nodding. "Yuuki told me that if you desired to know, I could tell you everything about her. Her hospital room is on the top floor of the center ward. It's a long hike, so we can talk as we go."

As she walked after the doctor, out of the lounge and toward the elevator, Asuna felt the same term repeating over and over in her head.

Terminal care. She felt that she had a very clear and simple idea of what that meant, but she didn't want to think that they would have such a direct term to refer to that "final" stage of life.

The only thing she knew for certain was that she needed to face and accept the truth that would be revealed to her soon. Yuuki allowed her to come into contact with her reality because she believed that Asuna could handle it.

In the lobby of the center ward building, there were three elevators. The rightmost said STAFF ONLY. The doctor ran the card he hung around his neck over the panel, and the door *bing*ed open at once.

They entered the box full of white glow, and the elevator began to ascend with almost no sound or sense of acceleration.

"Have you ever heard of the term *window period*?" Dr. Kurahashi suddenly asked. Asuna blinked and consulted her memory index.

"I believe...I learned that one in health class. Does it have something to do with virus...infections?"

"That's right. When a person is suspected of contracting a viral infection, you usually run a blood test. There's an antibody test, where you test the blood with antibodies that will react to the virus, and there's a more sensitive option called a NAT test that amplifies the virus's DNA and RNA. Even with the more powerful NAT test, it cannot detect a virus within the first ten days of infection. That time span is called the window period."

Dr. Kurahashi paused. They felt a very slight slowdown, and the door *bing*ed open again. The twelfth (and top) floor was prohibited to general visitors, and there was an imposing gateway right outside the elevator. The doctor ran his card over another sensor, then placed his palm on a panel for a biometric reading. The panel beeped, and the metal barricade bar sank out of the way. He motioned Asuna through the gate.

Unlike the lower floors, there were no windows in sight. It was just a long hallway with white panels and a left-right intersection up ahead.

Dr. Kurahashi took the lead again and turned down the left branch. The inorganic hallway, lit by soft white lights, continued on endlessly. They passed a few nurses dressed in white, but there was otherwise no hint of sound from the outside world.

"The existence of this window period inevitably gives rise to a certain phenomenon," the doctor said abruptly, continuing his earlier explanation, "and that is, the contamination of the transfusion liquid we collect through blood drives. Of course, the likelihood is very small. The probability of catching a virus from a single transfusion has to be one in hundreds of thousands. But modern medical science is unable to reduce that chance to zero."

He sighed faintly. Asuna felt a hint of helplessness in his mannerism.

"Yuuki was born in May of 2011. It was a difficult birth, and she had to be delivered by C-section. During the operation...it was unlabeled in the records, but there was some kind of accident that resulted in significant blood loss, requiring an emergency transfusion. And sadly, the blood that was used turned out to be contaminated with a virus."

"...!"

Asuna held her breath. The doctor glanced at her for an instant, then turned away and continued. "We don't know for certain at this point, but Yuuki was infected either at birth or shortly thereafter. Her father was infected within the month. The infection wasn't detected until September, via a post-transfusion blood test her mother received. At that point...it was too late for the entire family..."

He sighed heavily and came to a halt. There was a sliding door on the right wall, with a metal panel built into the wall next to it. The plate inserted there carried the imposing title of *First Special Instrument Room.*

The doctor slid his card through the slit below the panel. The machine *bing*ed and the door slid open with a hiss.

Asuna followed Dr. Kurahashi through the door, grappling with a pain like her chest was being wrung by a giant set of hands. The room was oddly long and narrow. On the far wall ahead was another door like the one they'd just passed through, and the right wall was lined with a number of consoles and monitors. The left wall was covered with an enormous horizontal window, but the glass was black, the space beyond invisible to her.

"The room on the other side of the glass is sterilized by air control systems, so I'm afraid you can't go in there," he said, approaching the black window and activating the control panel below it. The window hummed a bit, the dark color rapidly draining away until it was transparent enough to reveal the other side.

It was a small room. Actually, in terms of measurements, it was large. It only looked small because the space was crammed full of various machines. Some were tall, some were short, some were simple boxes, and some were rather complex. So it took her a little time before she noticed the gel bed at the center of the room.

Asuna got as close to the glass as she could, squinting at the bed. There was a small figure half sunken in to the blue gel. It was covered by a white sheet up to the chest, but the bare shoulders poking out above it were painfully thin. A number of tubes ran to the figure's throat and arms, connecting them to the array of machinery.

She couldn't see the face of the person on the bed directly. It was covered by a white cube, built into the bed, that swallowed almost her entire head inside of it. All she could see were thin, colorless lips and a pointed chin. There was a side monitor on the cube pointing toward them, shifting with a number of colored readouts. Above the monitor was a simple logo reading *Medicuboid.*

"...Yuuki...?" Asuna rasped. At last, she had found Yuuki in real life. But now that she was almost there, the last several feet were separated by a thick glass wall that could never be breached.

Without turning to him, Asuna timidly, hesitantly asked, "Doctor...what does Yuuki have...?"

His answer was short, but unbearably heavy.

"Acquired immunodeficiency syndrome...She has AIDS."

9

From the moment she saw the enormous hospital, Asuna was expecting something like this, the possibility that Yuuki was suffering from some terrible condition. But she couldn't prevent herself from gasping when she heard the name from the doctor's mouth. She stared through the glass at the prone Yuuki, feeling her body freeze solid.

This was the reality of it all? Both her reason and emotions refused to accept that the perpetually lively, powerful Yuuki was an isolated existence surrounded by imposing medical machinery.

I was a fool who didn't know anything and never tried to, a voice screamed inside of her. Now she knew the meaning of the tears Yuuki shed just before she vanished. They meant...

"But today, AIDS isn't nearly as terrible a condition as we once thought it was," she heard Dr. Kurahashi say kindly. "As long as you start treatment early after contracting HIV, you can hold off the onset of AIDS by ten or even twenty years. As long as you take your medicine and manage your health carefully, your life can be virtually the same as before contraction."

The doctor sat in the chair in front of the console with a small creak. He continued. "But, unfortunately, the virus she caught was a drug-resistant strain. Apparently, after it was revealed that the entire family was infected, Yuuki's mother considered having them all choose death. But she was also a devout Catholic. Through the power and support of her faith and husband, she was able to overcome the initial danger and chose to fight the disease."

"To...fight..."

"Yes. Just after she was born, Yuuki underwent HAART, or highly active antiretroviral therapy. After she survived the most critical early period, she grew up well, if a little small. She was relatively normal until elementary school, in fact. But it's difficult for a small child to take so many regular medications. And RT inhibitors have intense side effects. But Yuuki stayed strong and was determined to fight her condition. She hardly ever skipped a day of school, and she maintained grades that were the top in her class. She had many friends, and from what I've seen of the videos of that time, her smile was as radiant as the sun..."

He paused. Asuna heard him make a nearly inaudible sigh.

"Yuuki's status as an HIV carrier was kept secret from the school. That is normal protocol. Schools and businesses are forbidden from conducting HIV blood tests. But...right after she started fourth grade, through means unknown, a number of the school parents became aware that she was a carrier. The word spread like wildfire. The law prohibits discrimination against sufferers of HIV, but sadly, not every factor of society works solely on altruistic, healthy reasoning...The school was inundated with requests to remove her, as well as harassing letters and phone calls asserting all manner of false stories. Her parents resisted the onslaught of abuse, but ultimately, they had no choice but to move residences and transfer Yuuki to a new school."

"..."

Asuna couldn't even murmur to show that she was listening anymore. It was all she could do to listen to his words, her spine frozen stiff.

"But Yuuki continued to attend her new school without crying. However...life is cruel. It was just around this time that her

CD4 count, the lymphocytes that can indicate lowered immune response, began to drop precipitously. In other words...she had progressed to the AIDS stage. Even now, I believe it was the actions and statements of that school's parents and teachers, and the way they hurt her deep inside, that resulted in this shift."

The young doctor's voice was calm and measured. It was only the sharpness of his breath that betrayed his emotional state.

"When your immune system is compromised, it causes you to be vulnerable to viruses and germs that the body is usually perfectly capable of fighting. These are called opportunistic infections. Yuuki was first brought to this hospital when she contracted PCP, a particularly troublesome form of pneumonia. That was three and a half years ago. Even in the hospital, she was always smiling and reassuring us that she wouldn't give in and let the disease win. She never even raised a single complaint during the more painful tests. However..."

He paused briefly to shift his weight. "Germs and viruses exist everywhere, all over the hospital, and especially in the patient's body. So the risk of opportunistic infections continues even after hospitalization, and the longer you continue HAART treatment, the greater the risk that the virus will acquire more drug resistance. After the pneumonia, Yuuki caught esophageal candidiasis. This was right around the time that society was rocked by the NerveGear scandal. In the midst of calls to outlaw full-dive tech altogether, a medical-use NerveGear prototype developed by the government and tech companies—in other words, the Medicuboid—was installed in the hospital for clinical trials. But given that this was the *NerveGear*, and an even more powerful version at that, no one could have known the long-term effect it would have on the human brain. It was very hard to find patients who were willing to brave that risk to test the unit out. So with that in mind, I made a proposal to Yuuki and her family..."

As she waited for him to continue, Asuna stared at Yuuki on her bed, and the white cube that covered most of her face. The inside of Asuna's mind was cold and numb. What little of her confused wits was able to think straight desperately tried to avoid facing the truth.

Based on the time it was developed, the Medicuboid was an offshoot of the NerveGear, not the later AmuSphere. Asuna was totally used to the AmuSphere now, but there were times that she missed the greater, more immersive clarity of the original NerveGear's virtual reality. The AmuSphere had numerous safety measures, a lesson learned from the *SAO* Incident, but its simulation of reality was unquestionably inferior to the original device.

So the Medicuboid had several times the number of pulse nodes as the NerveGear, was capable of blocking signals from the entire body, and boasted a far more powerful CPU than the AmuSphere. Yuuki's incredible strength in Alfheim was a product of her interface, then?

An instant later, Asuna knew that wasn't true. The sharpness of Yuuki's skill far surpassed anything dependent on machine specs. In battle instinct alone, she was at least Kirito's equal, if not better.

As far as Asuna understood, Kirito's strength came from his experience fighting at the front line longer and harder than anyone else during his two years as a prisoner in *SAO*. In that case, how long had Yuuki spent inside the world created by the Medicuboid?

"As you can see, the Medicuboid prototype is an exceedingly powerful and delicate machine," Dr. Kurahashi said, after a long silence. "We installed it in this clean room for safe, long-term testing. In other words, conditions with no airborne dust or dirt, purged of all bacteria and viruses. In these circumstances, the test subject is at a vastly lowered risk of opportunistic infections. So I proposed this to Yuuki and her family."

"..."

"Even now, I wonder sometimes if it was really the best option for her. In AIDS treatment, we prize something called QOL: Quality of Life. It means trying to maintain a high-functioning, meaningful life for the patient during treatment. In that sense, the test subject has an inadequate QOL. She cannot leave the clean room nor come into contact with another human being. My proposal was a very difficult decision for Yuuki and her family. But I believe that the allure of the virtual world was what helped her make up her mind. She agreed to become a test subject and entered this chamber. Yuuki has been living inside the Medicuboid ever since."

"Ever...since...?"

"Yes, literally. She almost never returns to the real world. In fact, at this point, she *can't* return. In terminal care, we use morphine to ease the patient's pain, but she's currently getting that from the Medicuboid's signal-canceling function. Aside from her daily data collection test, which lasts a few hours, she's been traveling through various virtual worlds. My meetings with her happen over there, naturally."

"Meaning...she's been in a dive for twenty-four hours a day...? For..."

"Three years," he said.

She lost all words.

All this time, she assumed that it was the former *SAO* players who had the most AmuSphere experience of anyone in the entire world. But she was wrong. The tiny, emaciated girl on the bed over there was the purest traveler of virtual worlds on the planet. And *that* was the secret to Yuuki's strength.

You're a complete and total resident of this world, aren't you, Kirito had asked Yuuki. Through that short battle, he must have sensed something within her, something akin.

Somewhere in her heart, Asuna felt a sensation like humility flooding through her. She closed her eyes and lowered her head, feeling like a knight taking a knee and pledging her sword to a far superior warrior.

After a period of silence, Asuna tore her eyes away to face Dr. Kurahashi. "Thank you for letting me see Yuuki. She'll be just fine here, won't she? She'll be able to keep adventuring on the other side, won't she...?"

But he didn't respond at once. He simply sat in the chair in front of the console, hands folded over his knees, staring kindly at Asuna.

"Just being in a clean, sterilized room does not purge the bacteria or viruses inside her body. Such things only grow in strength as the body's immune system weakens. Yuuki is suffering from cytomegalovirus and nontuberculous mycobacterial infections—she's lost nearly all sight. She's also got brain lesions caused by the HIV itself. She's essentially unable to move her body on her own anymore."

"..."

"It's been fifteen years since she contracted HIV, and three and a half years with AIDS. Yuuki is in her terminal stage. She's recognized this fact with lucid understanding. I believe that you understand now why she wanted to vanish."

"No...no..."

Asuna shook her head. Her eyes were wide. But she couldn't cast aside the truth that had been laid upon her.

Yuuki had always resisted getting any closer to Asuna. In truth, it was for Asuna's own sake. Yuuki wanted it that way to minimize Asuna's pain when the inevitable parting came. And it wasn't just her. Siune and the rest of the Sleeping Knights had maintained that mysterious attitude whenever the topic came up because they knew the truth as well.

But Asuna never realized, never tried to learn, and ended up hurting Yuuki. With a sharp, stabbing pain, Asuna recalled Yuuki's tears before she logged out at Blackiron Palace. Suddenly, she realized something.

She looked up and asked, "Um, Doctor...did Yuuki have...an older sister?"

His eyebrows shot up in surprise. He hesitated but eventually nodded. "I didn't tell you this, because it doesn't pertain to Yuuki herself...but you are correct. Yuuki had a twin sister. That was the reason for the C-section that was the cause of all of this."

He looked up into empty space, perusing his memories, and grinned.

"Her sister's name was Aiko. She, too, was at this hospital. They weren't the most identical of twins...Yuuki was the happy and energetic one, and Aiko preferred to sit back and watch her. Now that I think about it...something about your face and mannerisms reminds me of her..."

His use of the past tense bothered her. She stared at him. He seemed to sense her unasked question, and explained, "Yuuki's parents died two years ago...and her sister died last year."

She thought she had understood what it meant to lose something.

Asuna had repeatedly witnessed the loss of human life while in that long-lost world. On several occasions, she had peered into that abyss herself. So she thought she understood that when the time came, people died. That no matter how hard you struggled, there were certain facts that could never be overturned.

But now that she understood the past and current state of Yuuki, a girl Asuna had only known for a few days, the weight of it overwhelmed her. She leaned against the thick glass. The very meaning of the word *reality* was melting, trickling away. She pressed her forehead against the cold, hard surface.

She had fought hard enough. Somewhere in her mind, she thought there was nothing wrong with fixating on the simple pleasure she had found. She made excuses for being afraid of change, shying away from friction, backing away and mincing her words.

But Yuuki had been fighting from the moment she was born. She fought and fought and fought against the cruel reality that threatened to steal everything she had, and even knowing her impending finality, she still found the strength to flash that radiant smile.

Asuna shut her eyes tight. Silently, she sent a message to Yuuki, who was undoubtedly traveling some far-off land right now.

I want to see you again. Just one more time.

She wanted to talk to her about the truth this time. Yuuki had told her that there were things she couldn't get across without confronting them. If she couldn't rip away everything that she'd wrapped around her weakness and exchange words with Yuuki again, then why had they met at all?

At last, something hot bled into the lids of her eyes. Asuna put her right hand to the glass window, tensing her fingers, seeking any kind of texture from its perfectly smooth surface.

Suddenly, from nowhere in particular, a gentle voice said, *"Don't cry, Asuna."*

Her head shot upward as if on a spring. Her eyes sprang open as well, droplets flying from her lashes. She stared at the bedridden girl. The little figure was still lying prone there, in the exact same spot she had been before. Nothing was different with the white machine covering her face. But Asuna noticed that one of the blue indicator lights on the side facing her was blinking irregularly. The display on the monitor was different from before—it was displaying a small message reading USER TALKING.

"Yuuki…?" Asuna murmured, barely a whisper. She tried once more, louder this time. "Yuuki? Are you there?"

The response was immediate. The speakers fixed above the thick glass partition had to be conveying her voice over there.

"Yeah. It's through the lens, but I can see you, Asuna. Incredible…You look just like you do over there…Thanks for coming."

"…Yuuki…I…I…"

The more she wanted to say, the less the words would come. She felt an indescribable helplessness wrench at her heart. Before her lips would work, the speakers above continued.

"Doctor, please let Asuna use the room next door."

"Huh…?"

Asuna turned around, confused. Dr. Kurahashi was deep in thought, his expression severe, but eventually he regained his usual gentle smile.

"Very well. On the other side of that door is the full-dive seat

and AmuSphere that I use for our meetings. You may lock it from the inside, but please keep yourself to twenty minutes or so. We are cutting out a number of steps here, after all."

"Er...of course," she replied hastily, then looked back at the girl lying beneath the Medicuboid. Yuuki's voice emerged from the speakers.

"ALO's included in the app launcher, so once you log in, come to where we first met."

"Okay...got it. Hang on, I'll be there soon," she said, her voice loud and clear. She gave Dr. Kurahashi a polite bow and turned to the door. Within a few steps, she reached the far wall of the monitor room and placed her hand over the sensor. When the door slid open, she squeezed through it.

The room beyond was about half the size of the monitoring station. There were two black leather recliners, both with familiar circular headgear on the headrests.

She impatiently turned back to lock the door, casting her bag onto the floor, then lay on the nearer of the seats. At the end of the armrest were some buttons that she used to adjust the incline, then she picked up the AmuSphere and set it on her head. Asuna took a deep breath, turned on the power, saw nothing but white, and left the real world.

Asuna awoke as the undine fencer in the bedroom of her forest home. She leaped upward without waiting for her VR senses to become fully aligned. Her wings buzzed as they carried her through the window without her feet touching the ground.

It was early morning in Alfheim, and the deep forest was shrouded in thick mist. She spun into a turn and then upward, shooting above the trees to break out of the layer of white. Her arms were held tight against her body as she rocketed toward the center of the floor.

In less than three minutes, she was within the airspace of the floor's main town, descending upon the glowing blue portal at the center of the square. As a number of players watched, wide-eyed, she did a half turn and came screeching to a stop. At the very moment that her bodily inertia hit zero, she passed through the gate.

"Teleport! Panareze!" she shouted. A deluge of pale light surged, pushing her upward.

In an instant, the process was done, and she hurtled out into the main plaza of Panareze, main city of the twenty-fourth floor. She jumped hard off the cobblestones, flying for the little island to the north of the city. Asuna zoomed at top speed, her shadow landing on the lake water wreathed with trails of mist.

The silhouette of a large tree loomed ahead. It seemed like the long-distant past in which Yuuki the Absolute Sword had waged her informal duels. The time she'd been there before, there had been a bustling crowd, but now it was empty and silent.

Asuna gradually slowed down, weaving around the trunk and preparing to land. The mist was so thick that she couldn't see the ground. She landed softly, rustling the dewy grass. Because it was still before dawn, her visibility was limited to just a few feet away. She raced around the tree, her desperation growing.

Halfway around the trunk, on the eastern side, a ray of light from the outer aperture finally broke through the mist for a moment. At last, through the break in the curtain, Asuna found the person she was looking for.

Yuuki was facing the other direction. Her long, dark hair and bronze-colored skirt waved in the breeze. As Asuna held her breath, the imp girl turned and stared at her with garnet-red eyes. Her pale lips formed a smile as delicate as melting snowflakes.

"For some reason, I just had a hunch that you'd find me in the real world. Even though you shouldn't have, since I didn't tell you a thing," Yuuki whispered, then smiled again. "But you came. It's pretty rare that my hunches come true. I was very happy... so happy."

Just a few days' absence had added a kind of transparency to

Yuuki's bearing. Asuna felt something sharp pinch her heart. She approached slowly, one step at a time, praying that the girl wasn't just an illusion.

Her extended fingers brushed Yuuki's shoulder. She was unable to stop herself from enfolding the girl's small body in her arms, squeezing her to feel the warmth.

Yuuki showed no surprise; she leaned her head against Asuna's shoulder like a blade of grass pushed by the wind. Through the contact of their bodies, Asuna felt a heart-trembling warmth from her that was greater than any digital data sent through electronic pulse nodes. She let out a slow breath and closed her eyes.

"...It smells the way it did when Big Sis would hold me like this. The smell of the sun..." Yuuki whispered, letting her weight lean against Asuna.

Asuna, meanwhile, uttered her first words here from trembling lips. "Do you mean...Aiko? Did she play VRMMOs, too...?"

"Yes. That hospital let us use AmuSpheres in ordinary patient rooms, too. Big Sis was the original leader of the Sleeping Knights. And she was way, waaay better than me..."

Yuuki ground her forehead into Asuna's shoulder. Asuna reached up and traced the silky hair. The younger girl tensed up, then eased. "At first there were nine Sleeping Knights. But we've lost three of them now, including Big Sis...So we all had a discussion and came to a decision. When the next one went, we'd break up the guild. But before then, we had to create the best memory ever...a great, fantastic adventure that we could tell Big Sis and the others about when we were reunited."

"..."

"We first met in a virtual hospice called Serene Garden, within a medical network. Our conditions are all different, but our circumstances are the same. So the server was set up for us to meet and have fun together in a VR environment, so that our last moments could be worthwhile..."

Ever since Dr. Kurahashi had started to explain back at the hospital, Asuna had a suspicion about this. There was that same strength, cheeriness, and calm that all of the Sleeping Knights shared; she had wondered if maybe that meant that they were all coming from the same place.

But even anticipating this bombshell, Asuna felt Yuuki's words sink to the bottom of her chest, irrevocably heavy. The bright smiles of Siune, Jun, Tecchi, Nori, and Talken all flitted through her mind's eye.

"I'm sorry, Asuna. For not telling you the truth. The Sleeping Knights aren't breaking up in the spring because we'll be too busy to keep playing the game. It's because two of us have been told that we have three months left at the most. So...so that's why we wanted to make our final memories here, in this wonderful place. We wanted to put proof that we had been here on that giant monument," Yuuki said, her voice trembling again. All Asuna could do was put more strength into her arms as she squeezed.

"But it wasn't really working for us...and we started to wonder if we should look for someone, just one person, who could help us. Not everyone was for it. They said that if whomever we chose found out the truth, it would be a burden on them and cause them terrible pain. And...that's exactly what happened. I'm sorry...I'm sorry, Asuna. If it's possible...I want you to forget about us. Right now, if you can..."

"I can't," she replied shortly. She rubbed her cheek against Yuuki's head. "Because it wasn't a burden, not in the least. It wasn't terrible. I'm so happy that I met you and was able to help you. Even now...I wish that you would let me join the Sleeping Knights."

"...Ahh..."

Both Yuuki's breath and her delicate body shuddered deeply for an instant. "I...I'm so happy I came here and got to meet you, Asuna...Just hearing that was enough for me. Now, at last...I'm satisfied...with everything..."

"..."

Asuna put her hands on Yuuki's shoulders and pulled away. She stared into those wet, shining purple eyes.

"But…but there are still so many things you haven't done. There are all kinds of places you haven't seen in Alfheim yet… and if you include all the other VR worlds, this place is endless. So please, don't say you're satisfied…"

She was trying her best to keep finding the right words, but Yuuki's gaze and smile were vacant, as though she were looking at something far, far away.

"In the last three years…we've gone on all kinds of adventures in all kinds of worlds. I want the memory I created with you to be the final page."

"But…there has to be more…More things to do, more places to go…" Asuna suggested desperately. If she didn't challenge Yuuki's decision, the girl might simply disappear into the mist in a moment. Suddenly, Yuuki's focus snapped from the distant horizon to Asuna's face, and she smiled in that mischievous way she'd done so often during their struggle against the boss.

"That's a good point…I want to go to school."

"S…school?"

"I've gone to school in the virtual world a few times, but it's too quiet and pristine and well-mannered. I want to go to a real school again, the kind I went to years and years ago," Yuuki said, grinning, then ducked her head in apology. "Sorry for asking the impossible. I really, really appreciate the way you feel. But I really am happy with this…"

"You might be able to."

"…Huh?" Yuuki blinked in surprise, then stared at Asuna. The older girl thought hard, trying to summon the memory from the back of her mind.

"I think you might be able to go…to school."

10

The next day, January 12th, 12:50 PM: On the north end of the third floor of Building Two, Asuna sat in a chair in the computing room far from the lunchtime bustle, her back straight.

There was a small domed machine, about three inches across, fixed to the right shoulder of her school blazer with a thin harness. The base was made of plated aluminum, but the dome was clear acrylic with a video lens inside. Two cables ran out of the base's socket, one traveling to Asuna's cell phone in her jacket pocket and the other to a small desktop PC on the table next to her.

At the PC, Kazuto and two other students in the mechatronics class with him were huddled together, exchanging mysterious tech terminology that sounded like magic spells or sorcerers' curses.

"I'm telling you, the gyros are too sensitive. If you're going to prioritize eye tracking, you need to allow the parameters to go a little looser..."

"But won't that cause major lag if there are any twitchy movements?"

"In that case, you'll just have to trust the learning capabilities of the optimization program, Kazu."

"Um, excuse me, Kirito? Lunchtime's almost over...!" Asuna

snapped, frustrated with being stuck motionless in the same position for more than thirty minutes. Kazuto looked up, letting out a thoughtful hum.

"Well, I think the initial settings should be okay now. Uh, can you hear me, Yuuki?" he asked, not to Asuna, but to the dome on her shoulder. Yuuki the Absolute Sword's cheerful voice piped up out of the speakers on the machine.

"Yes, I can hear you!"

"Good. We're going to initialize the lens area, so speak up when your field of vision becomes clear."

"Okay, got it."

The half-sphere piece of tech on Asuna's shoulder was called an "AV Interactive Communications Probe," and Kazuto's team had been testing it out since the start of the year. It was essentially a tool that allowed a user to see and hear distant locations in the real world through the use of an AmuSphere network. The lens and mic inside the probe collected data that were sent to the Internet through Asuna's phone, where they eventually reached Yuuki's full-dive space through her Medicuboid at Yokohama Kohoku General Hospital. The lens could swivel freely within the dome, synchronizing the visual source with the movement of her eyes. From Yuuki's end, it felt like she was a tenth of her original size, perched on Asuna's shoulder like this.

When Yuuki mentioned that she wanted to go to school, Asuna recalled this device, especially when she'd heard so many complaints about this particular research theme.

The lens whirred as the motors fine-tuned its focus, and when Yuuki said, *"There,"* they stopped.

"That should do it. There's a stabilizer on board, but try to avoid any sudden movements if you can, Asuna. And don't shout too loudly. Even a whisper will still carry over just fine," Kazuto explained.

"Got it, got it," she responded, stretching at last, then getting slowly to her feet. Kazuto pulled out the cable connected to the

PC. She spoke softly to the probe on her shoulder. "Sorry about that, Yuuki. I was hoping to show you around the school first, but now our lunch break is over."

Yuuki's voice emerged from the little speaker. *"That's okay. I'm really looking forward to sitting in on your class!"*

"Okay. In that case, let's go and say hello to the teacher for my next period."

She waved to Kazuto's team, who were all exhausted from their forced probe setup, and left the computing room. As she walked through the hall, descended the stairs, and crossed the bridge connecting the buildings, Yuuki exclaimed at each and every feature she noticed. But when they reached the door marked FACULTY ROOM, she fell silent.

"…What's wrong?"

"Umm…I've never been very comfortable around faculty rooms…"

"Hee hee! Don't worry, none of the teachers at this school are super teacher-y," Asuna whispered, laughing. She thrust the door open. "Pardon me!"

"Pardon meee."

With two echoing greetings, Asuna strode past the line of desks. The teacher in charge of fifth-period Japanese had been the vice principal of a middle school until retirement, and he volunteered to go back to work when this special, urgent education facility was arranged. He was in his late sixties but was adept at using the various network devices around the school, and he carried an intellectual bent that drew Asuna to like him.

She explained the situation, feeling relatively sure he would understand the circumstances, but felt a bit nervous all the same. The white-haired, white-bearded teacher listened with a large cup of tea in hand. When she finished the story, he nodded.

"Yes, that's fine. And what did you say your name was?"

"Oh, er…Yuuki. My name is Yuuki Konno," the probe responded instantly. This did seem to catch the teacher off guard, but his mouth crinkled into a grin soon after.

"Miss Konno, I would be delighted if you sat in on my class. We're about to cover Akutagawa's *Rail Truck*, and it doesn't get good until the very end."

"O-of course! Thank you, sir!"

Asuna thanked the teacher as well. The warning bell rang then, so she quickly stood up and bowed, then left the faculty room. The two girls breathed a sigh of relief. They shared a look and laughed, and Asuna rushed off to the classroom.

She was deluged with questions from her classmates as soon as she took her seat and they noticed the strange device on her shoulder, but an explanation of how Yuuki was in the hospital and a demonstration of its voice capabilities helped them understand how it worked right away. At that point, the other students started introducing themselves. Once it was finished, the bell rang again, and the teacher walked through the door.

At the prompting of the student on daily duty, the class was called to stand and bow—the little lens inside the probe whirred up and down—and the elderly teacher walked over next to the front desk, stroked his beard, and began the lesson, just like any other day.

"Ahem, please open your books to page ninety-eight, as we will be covering Ryunosuke Akutagawa's *Rail Truck* today. Akutagawa wrote this story when he was thirty years old…"

As the teacher spoke, Asuna brought up the appropriate section of the textbook on her tablet and held it up in front of her so Yuuki could see. But she nearly dropped it when she heard what the teacher said next.

"Now we're going to start this from the beginning. Would you like to read, Miss Yuuki Konno?"

"Huh?!" Asuna blurted.

"Y-yes, sir!" Yuuki stammered at the same time. The classroom was filled with hushed murmurs.

"Is it too hard for you?" the teacher asked. But before Asuna could speak up, Yuuki blurted out, *"I-I can read it!"*

The speaker on the probe had a powerful enough amp that

her voice reached the corners of the room. Asuna stood up with a start and held the tablet up to the lens with both hands. She twisted her head to the right and whispered, "Yuuki...c-can you read it?"

"*Of course. I'm a bookworm, believe it or not!*" Yuuki retorted. She paused, then clearly and enthusiastically began to read from the textbook: "*...The construction of the light rail between Odawara and Atami began in...*"

Asuna closed her eyes as she held up the text, concentrating solely on Yuuki's voice as it read with rich inflection. On the screen of her mind, she could see Yuuki, wearing the same school uniform as her, standing at the adjacent desk. Asuna was certain that this scene would one day come true. Medical science was making leaps and bounds by the year. In the very near future, they would develop a solution that wiped out HIV altogether, and Yuuki would be able to return to normal life soon after. Then they could truly walk hand-in-hand around the school and the city. They'd stop to get fast food on the way home, chatting about nothing in particular with burgers in their hands.

Asuna wiped her eyes with her left hand so that Yuuki couldn't see. The other girl was busy reading the century-old text with emotion and enthusiasm, and the teacher did not seem inclined to stop her. The post-lunch school was silent, as if the entire student population were listening to her read.

After that, they sat through sixth period as well, and when it was over, Asuna took Yuuki for a tour, as she promised. What she didn't expect was that more than a dozen classmates would join them, each clamoring to point out this or that to Yuuki.

Once they were alone again at last and sitting on a courtyard bench, the sky above was already turning orange.

"*Asuna...thank you so much for all of this. It was really fun...I'll never forget this day,*" Yuuki said out of the blue, suddenly serious.

Asuna automatically responded with cheer. "What do you mean? The teacher said you could come every day. Japanese class is third period tomorrow, so don't be late! More important, is there anything else you'd like to see? It can be anywhere outside of the principal's office."

Yuuki giggled, then fell silent. Eventually, she offered hesitantly, *"Um…there's one place I'd like to go."*

"Where?"

"Can it be outside of school?"

"Uh…" Asuna mumbled, thinking it over. The probe's battery would hold out for a while, and there was no reason she couldn't travel with it, as long as her phone got Wi-Fi. "Yeah, it's fine. I can go anywhere that I get signal!"

"Really?! Then…I know it's far, but…do you think you could take me to a place called Tsukimidai, in the Hodogaya ward of Yokohama?"

From western Tokyo, where the school was, Asuna and Yuuki rode the Chuo, Yamanote, and Toyoko lines on their route to Hodogaya in Yokohama.

They limited themselves to whispers on the trains, of course, but out in the open, Asuna freely conversed with the probe on her shoulder, unconcerned with what anyone else thought. The neighborhood had apparently changed in the three years that Yuuki was hospitalized, and so they stopped here and there wherever her interest was caught, explaining this and that feature.

Given that pace, when they finally got off the train at their destination of Hoshikawa Station, the big clock at the center of the traffic rotary outside showed that it was after five thirty.

Asuna looked up to the sky, which was transitioning from deep red to purple, and took a deep breath. The cold air here seemed to carry a different flavor than what was found in Tokyo, perhaps because of the nearby rolling hills covered in trees.

"It's a beautiful place, Yuuki. The sky's so clear and open here," Asuna said cheerfully, but the girl's response sounded apologetic.

"Yes…I'm sorry, Asuna. I shouldn't have forced you to come so far away…Will you be okay with your family?"

"Just fine! I'm always late to come back home," she replied

automatically, but in fact, Asuna hardly ever broke her evening curfew, and when it did happen, her mother was furious. But in this case, she didn't care how much trouble she would be in for being out late. She would take Yuuki as far as she wanted to go, as long as the probe's batteries held up.

"Just let me send a quick message," Asuna said lightly, taking out her phone. She opened the messaging app, taking care not to shut down the connection to the probe, and sent a message to her home computer explaining that she would be late returning. She was certain that her mother would send an angry message about breaking curfew, then a direct call, but if she kept her phone connected to the Net, it would automatically send the call to voice mail.

"That should do it. So, where do you want to go, Yuuki?"

"*Well, um...turn left at the station, then right at the second light...*"

"Got it."

Asuna began to walk, passing through the small shopping district outside the station in accordance with Yuuki's directions. With each bakery, fish market, post office, and shrine they passed, Yuuki made a wistful comment or two. Even into the following residential area, she was sighing and gasping at every house with an especially big dog or any tree with beautiful stretching branches.

It was easy for Asuna to understand that this was where Yuuki once lived, even without her saying so. No doubt the place they were heading at the moment was—

"*...When you turn up ahead, stop in front of the white house...*" Yuuki directed. Asuna noticed that her voice was faintly trembling. She turned right along a park lined with poplars bereft of their leaves and saw a house on the left side of the street with white tile walls.

She took a few more steps and came to a stop at the bronze front gate.

"..."

Yuuki let out a long sigh on Asuna's shoulder. Asuna absently lifted her left hand to trace the aluminum base of the probe with a finger as she whispered, "This…is your home, isn't it?"

"Yes. I didn't think…I'd ever see it again…"

The white-walled and green-roofed house was a bit smaller than the others in the neighborhood, but it had a larger yard. There was a wood table and bench in the grass, and beyond that was a large flower bed surrounded by red bricks.

But the table was faded from the sun and rain, and the only thing in the flower bed was desiccated weeds. Warm orange light poured out of the windows of the houses on either side, but all the storm shutters were closed on the little white house. There was no sign of life coming from it.

That was to be expected. Of the father, mother, and two daughters who once lived here, there was only one person left—and she was sealed in a special room, surrounded by machines on a special bed, never to leave again.

Asuna and Yuuki stared at the house in silence, its appearance lilac in the dying light of the day. Eventually, Yuuki said, "Thank you, Asuna, for taking me all this way…"

"Want to go inside?" Asuna asked, even though she knew it wouldn't look good to anyone on the street who might see her break in. But Yuuki sent the lens whirring left and right.

"No, this is enough. Well…let's get going, Asuna. You'll be late."

"If…if you want to stay here a bit longer, I don't mind," Asuna said automatically, then turned to look behind her. There was the park, bordered by narrow streets, with hedges set in stone beds running around it.

Asuna crossed the street and sat on one of the stone retaining walls at knee height. She turned so the probe could look right across the street at the hibernating little house. Yuuki could see the entire place clearly.

But after a brief silence, her companion quietly said, "It wasn't even for a year that I lived in this house, but…I do remember each and every day so vividly. We lived in an apartment before that, so having our own yard was just wonderful. Mama didn't like it because she was worried about infections, but Big Sis and I would run around on the grass...We ate barbecue on that bench, built a bookcase with Papa...They were fun times..."

"That's nice. I've never done anything like that."

Asuna's house had an enormous yard, of course. But she couldn't ever remember playing in it with her parents or brother. She was always playing house or drawing on her own. So she felt a longing for the family memories that Yuuki described.

"We should have a barbecue party at your cabin on the twenty-second floor then, Asuna."

"Yeah! It's a promise. We'll get my friends, and Siune and the others..."

"Oh boy, you'd better have plenty of meat ready, then. Jun and Talken will eat you out of house and home."

"Really? They don't seem the type to me."

The girls laughed, but then returned to gazing at the home.

"Actually...this house is causing a big rift among my extended family right now," Yuuki admitted with a tinge of sadness.

"A big rift...?"

"Everyone has their own ideas about what to do with it: tear it down and build a convenience store, sell the empty lot, or rent it out. In fact, Papa's older sister actually came and full-dived to talk with me about it. Which is funny, because they all avoided me in real life when they found out about my illness. She wanted me...to write a will..."

"..."

Asuna stopped breathing.

"Oh, sorry. I didn't mean to complain."

"N...no. Go ahead. You go and get it all off your chest, if you want." She barely managed to squeak it out, but Yuuki nonetheless made the lens nod on her shoulder.

"Okay. So...I told her, I can't hold a pen or press a seal in real life, so how am I supposed to write a will? She had no idea what to say to that." Yuuki giggled. Asuna cracked a brave grin.

"Instead, I told her that I wanted the house to stay as it is now. Papa's trust has enough money to pay upkeep for about ten years. But...I don't think it'll work. I think they're going to tear it down. That's why I wanted to see it, one last time..."

Asuna could hear the fine servos buzzing as Yuuki zoomed in and out on various features of the home. It seemed to her that it was the sound of Yuuki's memories being relived, and she felt her heart swelling to bursting, so she decided to just say what was on her mind.

"Okay...this is what we should do."

"Huh...?"

"You're fifteen, right? When you're sixteen, you're legally allowed to get married. Then you could have that person take care of the house for you..."

As soon as she said it, she saw the flaw. If Yuuki were in love with anyone, it would be one of the boys in the Sleeping Knights, but they were all dealing with fatal conditions of their own. Some of them had been given their final warning. So getting married wouldn't change things for the better; if anything, it would just get more complicated. Not to mention that getting married required two people to be on the same page...

But after a brief silence, Yuuki burst into wild laughter.

"Aha-ha-ha-ha! Asuna, you come up with some crazy ideas! I see; I never considered that one. Hmm, maybe that's not so bad. I bet I could try my hardest to fill out a marriage form! But sadly, I don't think I have anyone to marry," she said, still chuckling.

Asuna grimaced and said, "R-really...? You seemed to be awfully friendly with Jun."

"Oh, no way, not a little kid like him! Let's see...maybe..." She paused. Her voice grew mischievous. *"Hey, Asuna...would you marry me?"*

"Uh..."

"Oh, but you'll have to be the bride and take my name. Otherwise I'd be Yuuki Yuuki!" she said, giggling, but Asuna panicked. It was true that Japan had followed America's lead in engaging

the same-sex-marriage debate—the topic arose in the media a few times a year—but no serious political proposals had emerged yet, as far as she knew.

Yuuki gleefully said, *"Sorry, I'm just kidding. You already have a sweetheart of your own. It was him, right...? The one fiddling with the camera..."*

"Er...uh...yes, that's right..."

"You oughta be careful."

"Oh...?"

"I have a feeling that he lives somewhere apart from reality, just not in the same way I do."

"..."

Asuna tried to consider what Yuuki was saying, but her head was spinning too fast to make sense of it. She rubbed her heated cheeks and glanced over at the lens. Yuuki said kindly, *"Thank you, Asuna. Really. I'm so happy to have seen my old house again. Even if the house disappears, the memories will be here. The happy memories of Mama, Papa, and Big Sis will always be here..."*

Asuna understood that when she said "here"—it was referring not to the place where the house was but inside of Yuuki's heart. She nodded firmly, sending the message that the gentle, peaceful air of the house was already imprinted upon herself, too.

Her companion continued. *"When Big Sis and I complained and cried that it was too hard to take our medicine, Mama would always tell us about Jesus. She said that Jesus would never put us through pain that was so hard that we couldn't bear it. Then Big Sis would pray with Mama, but I would still be a bit upset. I always wanted Mama to talk to us in her own words, not the Bible's..."*

There was a brief pause. One big red star was blinking in the navy blue sky.

"But looking at the house again, I understand now. Mama was always talking to me as herself. It just wasn't in words...She was enveloping me in her feelings. She was praying for me so that I would keep walking forward, straight forward, without losing my way...I finally understand that now."

Asuna could imagine a mother and her two daughters kneeling at the window of the white house, praying to the starry sky. Guided by Yuuki's quiet voice, she felt herself putting feelings that had been lodged deep inside of her heart for years and years into words.

"You know...I, too...haven't heard my mother's voice in years. We sit and talk face-to-face, but I don't hear her heart. My words don't reach her, either. Remember what you said earlier, Yuuki? There are some things you can't get across without confronting them. How can I do it the way you do, Yuuki? How can I be as strong as you...?"

Perhaps they were cruel questions to ask of a girl who had lost her parents. Normally, Asuna would have simply been agreeable and not gone to the effort. But now, with Yuuki's strength and gentleness coming through the probe on her shoulder, Asuna felt the wall around her heart melting away.

Yuuki paused, answering her question haltingly. *"I...I'm not strong...at all."*

"That's not true. You're not like me at all: You don't base your actions on others, you don't shy away, you don't fall backward. You're just so...so natural about everything."

"Hmm...Actually, years ago, when I still lived in the outside world, I think I was always playing someone else. I could tell that Papa and Mama were secretly sorry that they had brought us into this world...So for their sake, I always had to be bright and energetic, to show them the sickness wasn't getting me down. Maybe that's why I can still only act that way in the Medicuboid. Maybe the real me would hate and blame everything, and spend all day crying about life."

"...Yuuki..."

"But you know what I think? I don't care if it's an act...Even if I'm only pretending to be strong, I don't mind at all, as long as it means more time that I'm smiling. You know I don't have much time left...I can't help but feel that whenever I interact with someone else, I'm wasting my time by holding back and trying to ascer-

tain indirectly how they feel. It would be better to just throw myself directly at them. And if they decide they don't like me, that's fine. It won't change the fact that I was able to get very close to their heart."

"…You're right…It's because of that idea that we were able to grow so close in just a few days, Yuuki…"

"No, that wasn't me. It was because you kept chasing, even when I ran away. When I saw and heard you in the monitoring room yesterday, I understood exactly how you felt about me. I knew that even after you learned about my sickness, you would want to see me again. I was…I was so happy, I could have cried."

Her voice hitched for a second, and there was a pause before she proceeded again. "So…maybe you should try talking to your mother the way you did back then. I think that if you really try to make your feelings heard, you'll get them across. You'll do fine; you're much stronger than I am. You are. If you don't confront her, you won't get your feelings across…And it was because you confronted me with your feelings that I felt safe in letting you know everything about me."

"…Thanks. Thank you, Yuuki," Asuna said, and tilted her head upward so the tears couldn't pool up and drip down her cheeks. The night sky, which never got truly black in the city, was full of stars that twinkled bravely through mankind's light.

Back at the train station, the battery alarm on the probe beeped. Asuna made a promise to Yuuki to take her to class again tomorrow, and then disconnected her phone.

By the time she had finished riding all the necessary trains back and was walking up to her home in Setagaya, it was after nine o'clock. The sound of the door unlocking echoed especially loudly in the chilly entryway.

Asuna took a deep breath. She could still feel the weight of Yuuki sitting on her right shoulder; she brushed it with her left hand to hold in the warmth, then took off her shoes and quickly headed for her bedroom.

As soon as she had changed out of her uniform, she exited into the hallway and walked to her brother Kouichirou's room. Like her father, Kouichirou was almost never home, but despite this assumption, she knocked anyway. There was no response. Just as she had done on the day that *SAO* launched, she opened the door without permission.

In the center of the fairly empty bedroom was a large business desk. She found what she was looking for on the left side: the AmuSphere Kouichirou used for attending VR meetings.

Asuna grabbed the headgear, which was quite a bit newer than hers, and took it back to her room. She inserted a memory card with the *ALO* client installed on it into a slot on the side of the unit. Once the headgear was adjusted to fit her head, she put on Kouichirou's AmuSphere and lay down on the bed.

After flipping on the power, the connection sequence booted up and took her to the login space for *ALO*. But Asuna chose to dive into *ALfheim Online* not with her usual account but a subaccount that she reserved for when she wanted to be somebody else.

She emerged in the living room of her forest cabin on the twenty-second floor. But this time she was not the familiar undine Asuna, but a sylph named Erika. She checked over her outfit, removing the double daggers she kept on her waist and stashing them in a storage chest. With that complete, she opened the menu and hit the temporary log-out button.

Just seconds after starting her dive, Asuna was back in her bedroom in the real world. She took off the AmuSphere, but the blue connection light was still blinking. This indicated that the connection to the VR world was in a suspended state, and if she hit the power switch with it on her head, she could return to the game without needing to log in again.

Asuna stood up with her brother's AmuSphere in hand. Thanks to their high-powered home Wi-Fi router, she could keep a solid connection from one end of the house to the other. She opened the door and went back into the hallway, descending the stairs with a heavier heart this time.

She peered into the living room and dining room, but the table was perfectly clean already, and her mother was nowhere to be seen. Farther down, around a turn in the hallway, light was peeking through the crack of the door at the end of the hall: her mother's study.

She stopped in front of the door and raised her hand, ready to knock, but hesitated multiple times before she could go through with it. Since when had it been so difficult for her to visit her mother's room? The truth was, it probably had as much to do with Asuna as it did with her mother. Her feelings weren't getting across because she wasn't trying to relate them. Yuuki had helped her realize that.

She thought she felt a small hand push her on the right shoulder, along with a voice.

It's all right, Asuna. I know you can do it…

Asuna nodded in agreement, sucked in a deep breath, and rapped on the door. She heard a faint voice beckon her in. She turned the knob, pushed her way through the doorway, and closed the door behind her.

Kyouko was sitting at her heavy teak desk, typing on the keyboard of a desktop PC. She continued tapping away for a time, then crisply smacked the return key and leaned back in her chair at last. When she pushed up her glasses and looked at Asuna, there was irritation there to a degree Asuna had never seen.

"…You came home late," she said simply. Asuna lowered her head.

"I'm sorry."

"I already cleaned up dinner. If you want to eat, you'll need to get something out of the refrigerator. And the deadline for that transfer school I told you about is tomorrow. Fill out that form by the morning."

She returned to the keyboard, signaling that the conversation was over, but Asuna had her statement ready.

"Actually, about that…I have something to say, Mother."

"Say it, then."

"It's hard to explain here."

"Then where can you explain it?"

Asuna walked up next to Kyouko rather than answering right away and handed her what she was carrying behind her back: the suspended AmuSphere.

"It's a VR world...I just want you to come with me somewhere."

Kyouko's brow furrowed with disgust the instant she caught sight of the silver headgear. She waved her hand to say that there was no room for discussion. "Absolutely not. I have no interest in hearing you say something that you cannot do me the respect of saying to my face."

"Please, Mother. I have to show you something. It will only take five minutes..."

Normally this was the point where Asuna would apologize and leave the scene, but this time she took a step forward, looking into Kyouko's eyes up close and repeating, "I'm asking you. I can't explain to you what I'm feeling and what I'm thinking while we're here. Please, just this once...I want you to see my world."

"..."

Kyouko glared at Asuna even harder, her lips tightly pursed. A few seconds later, she let out a long, deep breath.

"No more than five minutes. And no matter what you're going to tell me, I will *not* have you attending that school another year. When we're done, you will fill out that form."

"...Yes, Mother." Asuna obeyed, and held out the AmuSphere. Kyouko grimaced as she touched it and awkwardly placed it on her head.

"What do I do with this, now?"

Asuna quickly readjusted the fit for her and said, "When I turn it on, it will automatically connect you. Once you're inside, just wait until I show up."

Kyouko nodded her understanding and leaned back in the desk chair, and Asuna hit the power switch on the right side of the AmuSphere. The net connection light turned on, and the brain connection light began to blink irregularly. All of the tension went out of Kyouko's body.

Asuna rushed out of the study and ran up the hallway and the stairs back to her room. She plopped onto the bed and put on her own AmuSphere. When she touched the power switch, an array of light appeared before her eyes, ripping her mind from the physical world.

When she materialized in the wood-themed living room as her usual Asuna the undine, she looked around for Erika. Very quickly, she spotted the sylph girl with the short greenish hair standing next to the tableware cabinet, looking over her own appearance.

As Asuna approached, Erika/Kyouko glanced over her shoulder, glaring in the exact same way that she did in real life.

"It's all rather strange, that this unfamiliar face moves exactly the way I want it to. Plus..." She bounced up and down on her toes. "My body feels too light."

"Of course it does. That avatar's body weight is less than ninety pounds. It *should* feel different," Asuna said with a grin. Kyouko glared unhappily again.

"How rude. I'm not *that* heavy. Speaking of which...you seem to have the same face in here."

"Well...yes."

"But your real face is just a bit puffier in its outline."

"Now who's being rude, Mother? It's exactly the same in every way."

Asuna wondered how long it had been since she had a meaningless chat like this with her mother. She wanted to keep going for a bit longer, but Kyouko had her arms crossed in front of her chest, and meant business.

"All right, you're running out of time. What do you want to show me?"

"...Come this way," Asuna said, stifling a sigh as she crossed the living room toward the door to the little storage room that she used as an item repository. Once Kyouko had awkwardly tottered over, she showed her to a small window inside.

From the south-facing living room, there was a view of the large yard and the little path that traveled over hills and bumps until it reached the beautiful lake—a pastoral scene if there ever was one. But the only things visible from the north-facing storage room were the thick grasses around back, a little brook, and the close-hanging pine trees. During this season they were all covered in snow, leaving "cold" as the only apt description for the image.

But that was exactly what Asuna wanted to show Kyouko. She threw open the window and looked out at the deep forest.

"What do you think? Does it look familiar?"

Kyouko frowned again, then shook her head. "Familiar how? It's just an ordinary cedar fores…"

The words disappeared from her tongue. She stared out the window with her mouth open, but she was looking somewhere else, not at the scene before her eyes. At her side, Asuna whispered, "Doesn't it remind you…of Grandma and Grandpa's house?"

Asuna's maternal grandparents, Kyouko's parents, ran a farm in the mountains of Miyagi Prefecture. The house was in a small village nestled in a steep valley, and the rice paddies were carved right out of the mountainside, with no room for mechanization. It was mostly rice that they harvested, but even that was barely enough for the single family to live on for a year.

It was thanks to the forested mountain they inherited that the family was able to put Kyouko through college despite their humble income. The old wooden house was built up against the foot of the mountain, and when sitting on the back porch, the only things you could see were a small yard, a brook, and the cedar woods beyond them.

But more than the Yuuki mansion in Kyoto, Asuna had always preferred to visit her Grandpa and Grandma's house in Miyagi.

She would throw tantrums in summer and winter vacation until they finally took her, so she could lie under the same blanket as her grandparents and hear stories about the old times. She had many memories, from eating hand-shaved ice out back in the summer, to pickling plums with her grandmother in the fall, but what she remembered most vividly of all was plopping under the covered table in the wintertime, eating mandarin oranges and staring at the cedar trees through the window.

Her grandparents wondered what she found so entertaining about the woods, but something about the way the tall black trunks split the white of the snow in an endless pattern made her mind seem to float away. When she looked at the trees, she felt like a baby mouse in its burrow under the snow, waiting for spring—a strange sensation that was somehow both lonely and warm at the same time.

Her grandparents passed away one after the other when she was in her second year of middle school. The paddies and mountain were sold off, and without anyone to live in it, the home was torn down.

Which was why, in this house on the twenty-second floor of Aincrad, both physically and conceptually far removed from that little village in the mountains of Miyagi, Asuna felt a tear-jerking sense of longing whenever she stared out of the north window through the snowy conifers.

She understood that for her part, Kyouko did not look back on her poor rural upbringing with fondness. But Asuna still wanted to show her mother the view from this window—the view that she had once seen every day and was trying desperately to forget.

At some point, they passed the predetermined five-minute mark, but Kyouko was still gazing at the cedar trees. Asuna moved up next to her and said, "Do you remember the Obon holiday when I was in seventh grade? The time that you and Father and Brother went to Kyoto, but I was insistent on going to Miyagi instead, and so I ended up traveling on my own?"

"...I do remember."

"Well, I went so that I could apologize to Grandpa and Grandma. So I could apologize that you weren't able to come visit the family grave for the holiday."

"There was...a Yuuki family matter that I simply couldn't be absent from..."

"No, I'm not blaming you. You see...when I apologized, they brought out a thick album from the tea cabinet. I was amazed when I saw what was inside. It started with your first thesis, then all of the writings you submitted to various magazines, your interviews, all filed away. They even printed out the stuff on the Internet and stuck in it there. And I'm sure they didn't know the first thing about computers..."

"..."

"As he was showing me the things in the album, Grandpa said that you were their greatest treasure. You left the village and went to college, became a scholar, had your articles in fancy magazines, and were making a great name for yourself. He said you were so busy with your theses and meetings that it made sense you couldn't go back home for Obon to honor the dead, and they never once were upset about it..."

Kyouko was listening to Asuna's words in silence, staring out at the woods. There was no expression on her face, at least from the side. But Asuna kept pushing onward.

"And then he added, 'There might come a time when she gets tired and comes to a stop. She might want to turn back and see just how far she's come. And we'll always be here at this house, so she can find us...We've been keeping this little mountain home all this time, just so she knows that if she needs a source of support, she's always got a place to come back to.'"

As she spoke, Asuna saw her grandparents' old home, which no longer existed, in her mind's eye. And overlapping that, she saw Yuuki's little white house, from just a few hours earlier. A place for the heart to return. Even if they were physically gone, someone would always treasure them in their heart. And for Asuna, that place was this virtual cabin in the woods.

This home, too, would probably be obliterated someday. But in the truest sense, it would never be lost. A home wasn't a place to hold things, it was a word referring to the heart, feelings, way of life—the way that her grandparents had done.

"Back then, I didn't understand all of what he said. But recently, I feel like it finally makes sense to me. Running and running for your own sake isn't all there is to life…There must be a way of life that can make someone else's happiness into your own happiness."

She envisioned the faces of Kirito, Liz, Leafa, Silica, Yuuki, Siune, and the rest of the Sleeping Knights.

"I want to lead a life where I keep smiles on the faces of everyone around me. I want to lead a life where I can support those who are tired. And to do that, I want to strive for my best with studies and everything else at that special school I love so much," she finished at last, finding her words along the way.

But Kyouko only stared at the forest, her mouth shut tight. Her deep green eyes were looking far away, and it was impossible to gauge her true emotions at that moment.

For several minutes, the little room was silent. Two little animals that looked like rabbits frolicked and leaped in the snow beneath the large trees. They distracted Asuna for a moment, and when she looked back at Kyouko, she gasped.

A tear track was running down Kyouko's porcelain white cheek, dripping off her chin. Her lips budged, but no audible words came out. After a few moments, Kyouko realized that she was crying, and hastily rubbed at her face.

"What…Why is it…? I'm not crying…"

"…You can't hide your tears here, Mother. Nobody can stop from crying when they feel like crying."

"Well, that's inconvenient," Kyouko snapped, rubbing her eyes, then gave up and covered her face with both hands. Eventually, faint sobs emerged. Asuna hesitated several times, then finally reached out and placed a hand on Kyouko's trembling shoulder.

*　　*　　*

At breakfast the next morning, Kyouko was back to her normal self, reading the news on her tablet. The meal proceeded in silence after the morning greetings, and Asuna steeled herself for another demand for the transfer school form. Instead, Kyouko glared at Asuna with slightly less danger than usual and said, "So are you claiming that you're prepared to support someone else for your entire life?"

She nodded, surprised. "Y...yes."

"But if you want to support others, you need to be stronger yourself. You must go to college. And that means getting better marks than you have already, in the third term and next year."

"...Are you saying...I don't have to..."

"What did I say? It depends on your grades. So get on it."

With that, Kyouko got up and left the dining room. Asuna watched the door shut behind her, then lowered her head and thanked her.

She managed to maintain a somber mood as she dressed in her uniform and went to the door with her school bag, but as soon as she left the front gate, she started running down the gleaming, icy street. She couldn't keep the smile from breaking out over her face.

She wanted to tell Kazuto that she would still be at their school for the next year. She wanted to tell Yuuki that she'd finally had a real talk with her mother.

Asuna couldn't keep the grin off her lips as she raced through the crowds and toward the train station.

Three days later, as planned, they held a huge barbecue out front at the cabin.

In addition to Kirito, Lisbeth, Klein, Leafa, and Silica—the usual suspects—there was Yuuki, Siune, and the rest of the Sleeping Knights, and the racial leaders Sakuya, Alicia, and Eugene and their associates. They actually had to put together a food-hunting party to acquire enough ingredients to feed the thirty-strong guests.

Before they raised a toast, Asuna introduced the Sleeping Knights. She did not mention their conditions, but with Yuuki's blessing, she explained that they were a veteran band that traveled from VRMMO to VRMMO, engaging in a memorable finish here in *ALO* before they disbanded.

The stories about the mysterious seven-man guild that defeated the twenty-seventh-floor boss on their own and the Absolute Sword who bested more than sixty consecutive dueling foes had spread far and wide throughout the game. Sakuya and Eugene immediately commenced with their recruiting speeches. Yuuki politely refused, which was a good thing—if all of the Sleeping Knights joined a particular race's side as mercenaries, it could overthrow the current power balance of the nine fairy peoples. That would have a huge effect on the current progress of the Second Grand Quest, which was ongoing at the moment.

After the rousing toast, a storm of gluttony commenced, and Asuna ate, drank, and spoke with Yuuki the whole while. Over the course of the party, they decided that they should just go ahead and shoot for the twenty-eighth-floor boss as well, and the after-party turned into a conquering tour of the twenty-eighth-floor labyrinth. They even piled into the top floor of the tower and dispatched the large crustacean boss, which would be funny if it didn't sound like such a tall tale.

Unfortunately, the only names carved into the Monument of Swordsmen belonged to Yuuki, Kirito, and the few others who were party leaders, but the team made a pact to try the twenty-ninth-floor boss with just the Sleeping Knights again, and they called it a day.

Even as they continued their adventures in Alfheim, Yuuki participated in classes at school using the interactive probe. She visited the Kirigaya home in Kawagoe and also made a trip to Agil's café in Okachimachi.

Yuuki had been cautious of Kazuto at first, due to his eerie intuition, but as a fellow swordsman, they actually got along quite well once she finally talked to him. After that, they traded barbs over Sword Skill usage in *ALO* and even the different ways that the probe could be improved in real life; at times, this got on Asuna's nerves. The other Sleeping Knights got right along with Leafa, Lisbeth, and the others, and they had great fun planning big events as a group.

In February, Asuna and the Sleeping Knights defeated the twenty-ninth-floor boss as a single party, cementing their fame within all corners of Alfheim. In the middle of the month, there was a unified dueling tournament. Kirito blasted through the eastern block while Yuuki dominated the western, and the final match was broadcast on the Internet TV station MMO Stream to tremendous fanfare.

As countless players watched breathlessly, Yuuki and Kirito delivered a ferocious, stunning duel with endless major Sword Skills, including their own OSSs, for more than ten minutes. When Yuuki finally dispatched Kirito with her divine eleven-part skill, it caused a cheer that practically vibrated the entire planet.

For defeating the legendary Kirito—even without his dual blades—Yuuki was named the fourth champion of the dueling tournament, and the tale of the Absolute Sword surpassed the bounds of *ALO* to ricochet around the Seed Nexus.

In March, Asuna kept her promise to her mother by passing her final exams. With the probe on her shoulder, she joined Rika, Keiko, Suguha, and phone-based Yui on a four-day vacation to Kyoto. By this time, they had made the probe capable of handling multiple client streams at once, so Siune, Jun, and the others joined Yuuki in getting a tour of the city, which made the tour guide experience quite fulfilling.

The group was allowed to stay at the Yuuki family's vast mansion, and the money they saved by doing this allowed them to splurge on delectable Kyoto cooking. Unfortunately, flavor was one thing the probe could not transmit, so they heard plenty of cheeky complaints from their remote audience. Asuna had to promise them that she'd recreate the cooking in VR when she got back, and paid the price with some truly humbling practice experiences in her VR cooking program.

It all passed like a dream. Asuna and Yuuki shared a long, long journey, through the virtual and real world. There were so many more places to go, and Asuna believed that she would have plenty of time for all of it.

One day, close to April, a sudden cold front coming across the Sea of Okhotsk blanketed central Japan in an unseasonal snow. The thick carpet seemed to cover the hints of spring in the air, and the weak sunlight took its time melting the layer of snow.

That was when Dr. Kurahashi sent Asuna a message saying that Yuuki's condition had taken a turn for the worse.

11

As she stared at the brief message on her phone screen, Asuna repeated a single phrase in her mind, over and over:

That can't be.

It couldn't be. Yuuki had been active and assertive in all of their recent activities, and Dr. Kurahashi himself said that her brain lymphoma wasn't progressing. There were cases of HIV being successfully held at bay for more than twenty years now. And Yuuki was only fifteen…She was supposed to have so much time. This turn for the worse was just another case of opportunistic infection, and she would survive it the way she had before, several times already.

But another part of her knew what it meant. It was the first time the doctor had sent her a message directly. It meant The Time had come—The Time that she had trembled in fear of every night until she convinced herself it wasn't true.

Asuna froze for several seconds, trapped between two arguing voices, then squeezed her eyes tight. She booted up her mail program, sending a short group message to Kirito, Lisbeth, Siune, and the others of their little group of friends. Once that was done, she changed out of her home wear and automatically chose her school uniform to save her the trouble of picking something out. She raced out of the front door with her shoes barely on, where the gentle afternoon sun reflected bright and white off the remnants of snow on the street and into her eyes.

It was two o'clock on a Sunday at the end of March. Everyone on the street walked slowly, as if savoring the long-awaited arrival of spring. Asuna ran hard toward the station, weaving her way around the pedestrian traffic.

Later, she couldn't even recall checking the train times and the travel thereof. The next thing she knew, she was racing through the gate of the station closest to Kohoku General Hospital. It felt like the inside of her head was fogged out with a light blur; scattered pieces of thought rose to consciousness and faded.

Hang on, Yuuki, I'm coming, she thought to herself, teeth clenched, as she darted toward a taxi pulling around to the curb outside the station.

Her visit had already been cleared ahead of time at the front desk of the hospital. When Asuna tensely informed the nurse of her reason for visiting, she received a guest card at once and was told to hurry to the top floor of the center ward.

She waited through the elevator trip, impatiently watching the number crawl upward one at a time, then leaped out as soon as the door opened. She practically slammed the card against the security gate sensor and resumed running, knowing that it was terribly bad hospital manners. As she followed the blank white corridor route by memory, the door to Yuuki's clean room came into view around the final turn.

And she came to a stop, her eyes bulging.

Of the two doors there, the first one was the entrance to the monitoring room. And the one in the back with the huge warnings and caution signs was the door to the air-sealed clean room. It had been, naturally, shut tight when Asuna visited before, but now it was wide open. As she watched helplessly, a nurse in completely ordinary garb quickly approached.

When she saw Asuna, the nurse nodded and whispered,

"Inside, hurry," as she walked past. At this prompt, Asuna took several unsteady steps toward the inner doorway.

Her eyes were stunned by the pure white of the room. The huge array of machines that had filled it before were all pushed up against the left wall. Two nurses and a doctor were standing next to the gel bed in the center of the room, watching over the small figure lying on it. All three were wearing their normal white uniforms.

As soon as she saw this, she understood. It had reached the stage of no return. The Time had come, as was preordained many years ago, and she had no choice but to watch it happen.

Dr. Kurahashi looked up and recognized Asuna immediately. He beckoned her over, and she worked her limp legs just enough to carry her into the room.

It was only a matter of feet to reach the bed, but it felt like an eternity. Asuna struggled onward, each step carving down the distance toward cruel reality, until she stood at the side of the gel bed.

A skinny girl lay there, covered in a white sheet up to her neck, her gaunt chest slowly rising and falling. The EKG over her left shoulder showed a green wave that pulsed weakly.

The rectangular Medicuboid that had covered most of her face before was now split into two parts. The part from her ears upward was tilted backward ninety degrees. The interior was molded into the shape of a human head, and it nestled the face of the sleeping girl.

In real life, Yuuki was painfully emaciated and so pallid she was nearly transparent. But something about her appearance struck Asuna as being almost mysterious in its beauty. It made her believe that if fairies were real, they might look like this.

She watched Yuuki in silence, until eventually Dr. Kurahashi appeared at her side and said quietly, "Good...I'm glad you made it in time."

Asuna didn't want to acknowledge the phrase *in time*. She

looked up swiftly and angrily at the doctor, but the intelligent eyes behind his glasses were full of nothing but sympathy. He spoke again.

"Her heart stopped temporarily, forty minutes ago. We were able to regain a pulse with some drugs and the defibrillator, but I'm afraid that...the next time might not..."

Asuna held her breath, then hissed through clenched teeth. But she wasn't able to form a complete, coherent sentence.

"Why...why is...I mean...I mean, Yuuki still..."

The doctor nodded kindly, then shook his head side to side. "As a matter of fact, when you visited in January, this day could have happened at any time. Between the fever from HIV wasting syndrome and the development of her primary central nervous system lymphoma, Yuuki's life has been hanging in the balance. She's been walking on thin ice. But she fought harder than we ever thought possible these last three months. She's been winning a fight with desperate odds for days and days and days at a time. She's fought harder than she ever needed to...No, in fact..."

For the first time, his voice broke slightly.

"In fact, these fifteen years of life for Yuuki have been one long, long fight. She's been fighting not just against HIV...but against cruel, unfeeling reality. I'm certain that the clinical test of the Medicuboid put her through an immeasurable amount of pain. But...she fought through it. If it wasn't for her, practical usage of the Medicuboid would be at least a year behind where it is now. So let's allow her to be at peace..."

As he talked, Asuna sent a silent message to her friend.

You won't let this beat you, Yuuki. I mean, you're the Absolute Sword...The greatest combatant alive, the girl who can cut anything in two. You won, Yuuki. You beat the disease...and fate...

At that moment, Yuuki's head twitched. Her pale eyelids fluttered and rose for just a moment. The gray eyes, which were supposedly already blind, took on a clear light and looked straight at Asuna.

Her lips, practically the same color as her skin, moved nearly imperceptibly. Her fragile hand twitched beneath the sheet, slowly, slowly extending toward Asuna.

His voice choked with emotion, the doctor said, "Asuna…take her hand."

Before the words were all the way out of his mouth, she was reaching out with both hands, enveloping Yuuki's bony hand in hers. The cold skin squeezed at her fingers, seeking something.

In that instant, Asuna received a revelation. She understood what Yuuki really wanted.

Still holding the girl's hand, Asuna looked up and quickly asked, "Doctor…can we use the Medicuboid right now?"

"Er, well, if we power it on…But…Yuuki said that she wanted her final moments not to be in the machine…"

"No, Yuuki wants to go back there now. I can tell. Please…let her use the Medicuboid, Doctor."

He stared at her for several seconds, then acquiesced. He gave a few orders to the nurses, then grabbed the side handle of the Medicuboid and carefully rotated the top half until it covered Yuuki's face.

"It will take about a minute to power up…What about you?"

"I'll use the AmuSphere in the room next door!" Asuna said, squeezing Yuuki's hand one last time before placing it back on the bed. She whispered a brief reassurance and turned away.

Through the clean-room door and into the monitoring station, there was a rear wall with a door in it. She leaped onto one of the two seats in the room beyond that door, picked up the AmuSphere from the headrest, and placed it on her crown. Even as she hit the switch and waited for the start-up sequence, Asuna's mind was already in that other world.

When she awoke in the log cabin, she jumped out the window and flew toward the city at max speed, the same way she'd done the last time she logged in from the hospital. As she flew, she opened her window and sent messages to Lisbeth, Siune, and the others, who she had on standby just in case.

Upon flying through the teleport gate, she immediately called out for Panareze. No sooner had she appeared in the lake-bound city than she buzzed away in the direction of the little island. Toward the foot of the tree where they first met.

It was evening in Aincrad. The setting sun shining through the outer walls lit the lake surface gold. She followed that band of golden light to the air over the little island, went into a steep descent, and landed on the soft grass.

There was no need to search around the tree this time. Yuuki was standing at the exact spot where they had traded blows, what seemed like so very long ago. The imp swordsman turned slowly, the chilly air rustling her long, dark hair.

When she saw Asuna approaching, Yuuki grinned. Asuna returned it.

"Thank you, Asuna. I forgot one very important thing. I wanted to give you something. So I was hoping to meet you here one last time."

Her voice was as cheery as ever, but with just the faintest hint of a quaver. Asuna understood that it was taking all of the energy Yuuki had left to stand here and talk to her.

She strode over to Yuuki and said, just as brightly, "What is it? What do you want to give me?"

"Well…Hang on, I'm going to make it now," Yuuki said, grinning. She opened her window and briefly fiddled with it. When it closed, she drew the sword at her waist. The obsidian blade seemed to burn in the setting sun. She held it out straight in front of her, facing the trunk of the tree. She paused there, stilled. It was as if she were gathering her last bit of strength into the point of the sword.

Her side profile twisted in agony. Her upper half swayed, but her legs were spread wide for balance, and they held firm.

She wanted to say that it was okay, that there was no need. But Asuna just bit her lip and watched instead. A breeze rustled the grass, then stopped. That was when Yuuki moved.

"*Yaah!*"

With a ripping cry, her left hand flashed. Five thrusts into the tree trunk, from right down to left. The sword zoomed back, then thrust five more times from left down to right. There was an explosion with each thrust, and the sky-splitting tree shook to its core. It would have been broken in half without a doubt, if it wasn't designated an indestructible part of the scenery.

With ten thrusts finished, Yuuki's body tensed again, and her blade darted at the intersection of the two lines. Blue-purple light shot in all directions, spraying the grass at her feet outward in a circle.

Even when the gust of wind had subsided, Yuuki stayed still, with the point of her sword touching the trunk. Then a small, rotating crest appeared around the point. A square piece of parchment was generated right out of the surface of the tree, absorbing the glowing blue crest and rolling itself up tight into a scroll.

Yuuki pulled the sword away, leaving the finished scroll floating in midair. She slowly reached out and took it.

With a faint *clank*, the sword dropped into the grass. Then Yuuki's body tilted and collapsed. Asuna rushed over and propped her up, crouching and picking up the little body with both arms.

Asuna was startled at first to see that Yuuki's eyes were closed, but the lids lifted soon after. Yuuki smiled serenely and whispered, "It's weird...I'm not in any pain at all, but I just feel weak..."

The older girl grinned back and said, "It's all right, you're just tired. You'll feel better if you get some rest."

"Yeah...Asuna...take this...It's my...OSS..."

Unlike just a moment ago, her voice was halting and broken. Realizing that Yuuki's final refuge—that the brain that kept her consciousness attached to the game—was losing its last bits of strength, Asuna felt a storm of emotions rip through her heart, but she suppressed them and smiled once again.

"You're really giving it to me...?"

"I want you...to have it...Now...open your window..."

"...Okay."

Asuna waved her left hand to call up the menu, then opened the OSS settings window. With the scroll trembling in her hand, Yuuki placed it against the surface of the floating screen. The parchment vanished in a twinkle of light, and Yuuki sighed in relief and dropped her hand. With an uneven smirk, she just barely croaked out, "The name...of the attack...is 'Mother's Rosario'...I'm sure...that it...will keep you...safe..."

At long last, the tears Asuna had been keeping at bay broke forth and spilled on Yuuki's chest. She never lost her smile, though, and said clearly, "Thank you, Yuuki. I promise: If the time ever comes that I leave this world for another, I will give this attack to someone else. Your sword...will never, ever be lost."

"Yeah...thanks..."

Yuuki nodded. Her amethyst eyes were wet and shining.

At that moment, a number of faint vibrations—the sounds of fairy flight—came into hearing range. They grew louder and louder, until eventually a series of boots hit the nearby grass. Asuna looked up to see Jun, Tecchi, Talken, Nori, and Siune approaching.

They formed a circle around Yuuki and fell to their knees. Yuuki looked at the group and smiled with consternation. "Come on...I thought we had our...farewell party already. You promised...not to...see me off..."

"We're not seeing you off, we're lighting a fire under you. We don't want our leader moping while she waits for us in the next world," Jun said, smirking. He squeezed Yuuki's hand in his burnished gauntlets. "Don't wander around when you get there, just wait. We'll be there before you know it."

"Don't...be silly...I'll be mad...if you show up...too soon."

Nori clicked her tongue to chide Yuuki and declared, "Nope! You're totally helpless without us around, Boss. You've got to be a good girl and wa...wait..."

Suddenly, Nori's face crumpled, and tears began falling from her big black eyes. A few sobs tore their way out of her throat.

"Don't do this, Nori...We promised we wouldn't cry..." Siune said with a smile, but there were two gleaming tracks on her cheeks as well. Talken and Tecchi joined in by grabbing Yuuki's hands, not even trying to hide their tears.

She looked around at her friends, put on a brave, tear-streaked face, and said, "Oh, fine...you guys...I'll be waiting...so just... take your time..."

The six Sleeping Knights all held hands in a ritual promise of understanding that they would meet again one day. Just as the other members of the team were getting back to their feet, the fresh humming of more wings approached.

This time it was Kirito, Yui, Lisbeth, Leafa, and Silica. They were running over as soon as they landed, joining the circle around Yuuki and taking turns clasping her hands.

As she cradled Yuuki in her arms and watched the scene through blurred eyes, Asuna noticed something odd. Even after this fresh group arrived, the buzzing of wings did not cease. And it wasn't one pair—it was a veritable pipe organ medley of count-less wings belonging to all the fairy races.

Asuna, Yuuki, Siune, Lisbeth, and all the others looked up into the sky. There they saw an especially thick ribbon stretching toward them from the direction of Panareze.

Dozens of players were flying together in a great line. At the lead, her long robe trailing in the air, was Lady Sakuya, leader of the sylphs. Behind her was a retinue of her fellow people, all clad in various shades of green. Based on the number, it had to be nearly the entire population of sylph players currently logged in to the game.

And they weren't just coming from the town. From all direc-tions of circular Aincrad, a variety of colored bands was descend-ing toward the little island. The red ribbon was the salamanders and the yellow was the cait siths. Imps, gnomes, undines... battalions of player races, led by their lord and ladies, were head-ing straight for the tree. There had to be at least five hundred...if not a thousand.

Yuuki gasped in wonder from her position in Asuna's arms. "Wow...it's incredible...Look at all...those fairies..."

Asuna beamed down at her and said, "I'm sorry, Yuuki. I figured you wouldn't like it...but I asked Liz to call for all of them to come anyway."

"I wouldn't like it? That's not...true at all...But...but why so many, all at once? I feel like...I'm dreaming..." she rasped. Meanwhile, the swarm of warriors hovering and descending onto the island was causing a roar of sound akin to a waterfall. The big groups, led by Sakuya, Alicia, and the other leaders gave Asuna's little group some breathing room as they took positions, kneeled on the grass, and bowed their heads in respect. The tiny island was soon completely covered by players.

Asuna stared into Yuuki's eyes and tried to put the emotions filling her chest into words.

"I mean...I mean..." The tears dripped again. "Yuuki...You're the greatest fighter to ever set foot on this world...We'll never see another person like you again. We can't just let you go off feeling lonely. Everyone here is praying for you...Praying that your new journey takes you somewhere just as wonderful as this."

"...I'm so happy...So, so happy..." Yuuki said, lifting her head so she could survey the crowd around them, then falling back against Asuna's arms again. She closed her eyes, her tiny chest taking several deep breaths, then opened them to stare at Asuna with those purple eyes. She sucked in deep, and with the last bit of her strength remaining, managed to squeeze out more words.

"I've...always wondered. If I were born into this world just to die...then why do I exist at all...? I can't create anything or provide anything...I just waste all these fancy drugs and machines... and make things harder for the people around me...And that just makes me feel worse...So I thought, over and over...if I'm meant to just vanish in the end...I ought to just disappear right now...I always wondered...why I am...alive..."

The very last drop of fuel that powered Yuuki's life was burning up before their eyes. The little body in Asuna's arms grew lighter and seemingly transparent. Her voice was so frail and halting, but the words she spoke hit Asuna in the center of her soul like no other words ever had.

"But...you see...I think I finally...found the answer...You don't need...a meaning...you just live...I mean...just look at how...fulfilling my final...moment is...Surrounded by...so many people...in the arms of...someone I love...at the end of my...journey..."

Her words ended on a short breath. Her eyes saw through Asuna, yearning for some place far, far away. Perhaps she really was heading for another realm—the true isle of fairies where the souls of heroes went to rest.

Asuna couldn't stop the tears from flowing. The drops spilled from her face and sparkled in the light on Yuuki's chest, but a smile rose to the girl's lips without prompting. Asuna nodded deeply and gave Yuuki her final message.

"I...I promise that I will see you again. In a different place, in a different world, I will come across you again...And when I do...you can tell me what you found..."

In that moment, Yuuki's purple eyes caught Asuna's. For a single instant, deep within them, there was a brilliance of unlimited life and courage, just like when they'd first met. That light turned into two drops that overflowed, spilled down Yuuki's white cheeks, and vanished into a spark of light.

Her lips barely budged, forming a smile. Inside her head, Asuna heard the voice:

I did my best to live...I lived here...

Like the last flake falling upon a pristine field of snow, Yuuki the Absolute Sword closed her eyes.

12

She felt something on the right shoulder of her uniform, and looked down to see a single, pale pink petal stuck to the fabric.

Asuna carefully reached over and plucked it off, cupping it in her palm to get a look. The beautiful, elliptical petal was pristine in appearance, trembling in place as though it had something to say, until the breeze finally lifted it off her hand to join the countless spots of white dancing in the air. She returned her hands to her knees and looked up at the hazy spring sky again.

It was three o'clock on the first Saturday of April. The memorial service for Yuuki, who had passed a week earlier, had just let out. The Catholic church in the hilly region of the Hodogaya ward of Yokohama was surrounded by rows of cherry blossom trees, which were letting their flowers drop in an apparent send-off. But the actual service was anything but reserved. Including the aunt who served as chief mourner, there were only four relatives of Yuuki's in attendance, but the number of friends in their teens or twenties numbered easily more than a hundred. Naturally, they were almost all *ALO* players. After three whole years in the hospital, her relatives must have assumed that Yuuki had no real friends close enough to pay their respects anymore, and they were stunned by the convoy that arrived.

After the service, the procession stuck around in the large

courtyard of the church in little groups, reminiscing about the Absolute Sword. For some reason, Asuna didn't feel like joining in. Instead, she found a bench around the back of the chapel in the shade and looked up at the sky by herself.

It was very hard for her to accept that Yuuki no longer existed in this world—not cheering through the probe on her shoulder or smiling ravenously at Asuna's home cooking in the forest cabin, but gone to a far-off realm, never to return. Her tears had run dry at last, but every now and then she imagined she heard Yuuki's voice in a crowd, the corner of a café, or on the breeze in Alfheim, and it never failed to make her heart skip a beat.

She was getting into the habit of thinking about life nowadays.

How many decades ago had it been that the world was shaken by the assertion that life was nothing more than the carrier of genetic code, a mission to reproduce one's own information and leave it behind to thrive? From that perspective, the HIV virus that had tortured Yuuki for all those years was a terrific example of pure life. But the virus within her, which had run rampant and successfully reproduced over and over, only succeeded in taking the life of Yuuki, its host, causing itself to die as well.

Depending on your point of view, mankind had been doing the same thing for millennia. At times, we took many lives in the search for personal gain, and our countries sacrificed other countries for the sake of safety. Even now, as she looked up, fighter jets taking off from Atsugi Base for some destination or another were leaving exhaust trails in the hazy spring sky. Would the time come that mankind destroyed the very world we lived in, just like a virus? Or would we fall prey to a different type of intelligent life in the competition for survival...?

Some of Yuuki's final words still echoed in Asuna's ears: *I can't create anything or provide anything.* In that sense, she did indeed leave the mortal plane without leaving her own genes behind.

But, Asuna thought as she touched her uniform ribbon, inside her heart, thanks to the briefest of encounters, Yuuki had succeeded in etching her existence in a deep and unforgettable way.

The gallant figure of the Absolute Sword, standing brave and tall against impossible odds without backing down—Yuuki's very soul—was alive and breathing. It was true of all hundred-plus youngsters here today. Even if time slowly broke down the memories bit by bit, crystallizing what remained, it meant that *something* was staying behind.

That meant that life wasn't just a genetic code written in four nucleobases, but also contained memories, mentality, and the soul. Not in the vague conceptual sense of a meme or imitation. One day in the future, when there would exist a medium that could accurately, easily record the mind itself, perhaps that would be the one big key to protect against the obliteration of the imperfect human species...

Until that day comes, I will continue to spread Yuuki's heart in whatever ways I can. And when I have children, I'll pass on the story—the story of the sparkling, miraculous girl who fought between the borders of the real world and the virtual, Asuna thought to herself. She slowly opened her eyes again.

She noticed a figure coming around the front corner of the building toward her and hastily rubbed at her eyes to wipe away the tears.

It was a woman. For a moment, Asuna thought she recognized her, but the facial features were unfamiliar. She was tall, wearing a simple black one-piece with a shawl. She had straight black hair that fell to her shoulders, with a thin silver necklace hanging over her chest the only accessory. She seemed to be in her early twenties.

The woman walked straight toward Asuna, then stopped a little ways away to bow. Asuna quickly stood and returned the courtesy. When she looked up, she was caught off guard by the blinding white of the woman's skin. The bloodless look of that skin reminded Asuna of how she herself had looked when she woke up from her long, long sleep. And now that she got a better look, the neck and wrists were thin enough to break with a simple brush of the hand.

The woman stared at her for a while, and then her beautiful, date-shaped eyes softened. A gentle smile appeared on her lips.

"You must be Asuna. You look just the same as over there, so I recognized you at once," she said, and Asuna realized who it was immediately, based on the clammy tone of voice.

"Oh...are you...Siune?"

"Yes, that's right. My actual name is Si-Eun Ahn. It's nice to meet you...and been a while."

"It's n-nice to meet you, too! I'm Asuna Yuuki. I suppose it's been a week, hasn't it?"

Their greetings were somewhat contradictory, a phenomenon that made them giggle when they realized it. Asuna motioned to the bench and joined Si-Eun.

At that point, Asuna belatedly realized something. The Sleeping Knights were supposed to be patients fighting incurable diseases, and at the terminal care stage of treatment. Was it safe for her to be walking around outside and alone like this?

Si-Eun perceptively sensed Asuna's concern and nodded very slightly. "It is all right. They finally gave me permission to venture outside this month. My brother is here attending to me, but I asked him to wait around the front."

"Then...you mean...your body is already...?"

"That's right...I have acute lymphoblastic leukemia...I contracted it about three years ago. Chemotherapy knocked it into remission...meaning that the cancerous white blood cells disappeared from my body, but it returned last year...After the recurrence, they said a bone marrow transplant was my only effective treatment. But no one in my family had the right HLA match for me...They couldn't find a donor at the bone marrow bank, either. I made my peace with this a long time ago and decided to live what time I have left to the fullest, but..."

Si-Eun paused, looking up at the cherry trees over her head. A tiny whirlwind sent up a spout of pink petals that flurried like snow.

"If a marrow transplant can't be attempted after recurrence, they can seek remission through a combination of drugs in what's called salvage therapy. They use new drugs, test drugs—anything they can come up with—so the side effects are severe... It was so painful that I wanted to give up many times. I wanted to tell the doctors that if there was no hope, I wanted to switch to a treatment that would make my remaining time easier..."

When the storm of cherry petals brushed at Si-Eun's hair, Asuna realized that it was a wig.

"But...whenever I saw Yuuki, I remembered not to give in. She was fighting the same suffering for fifteen years, so what was an older woman doing crying about a measly three? At least, that's what I told myself. Then, my medications started waning off in February...and the doctor said that my numbers were getting better, but I could tell that it was my time. They must have switched me from salvage therapy to QOL. That was scary, of course...but also a relief. I had heard about Yuuki's condition... so I knew that I could go anywhere with her. That no matter where we went, she would keep me safe...It's really quite silly of me to be so dependent on a girl much younger than me—"

"No...I understand that feeling," Asuna interjected.

Si-Eun smiled and continued. "And yet...a week ago, the day after we said good-bye to Yuuki, the doctor came to my hospital room...and said that I was in full remission, meaning all of my cancerous white blood cells were gone, and I could leave the hospital. I wondered what he meant. Was it just a temporary leave so I could spend time with my family? I was still confused when I was discharged from the hospital the next day. It was only yesterday that I considered that maybe my illness was cured. It seems that one of the test drugs worked wonders..."

Si-Eun paused and scrunched up her face into what looked like a combination of smiling and crying. "It just doesn't feel real yet. When your lost time is just handed back to you, you don't know what to do. Plus...there's Yuuki..."

Her voice trembled, just barely. Asuna felt a lump in her throat when she noticed there were little tears hanging in the corners of Si-Eun's eyes.

"Is it right for me to stay behind like this…when Yuuki is waiting up ahead…? Yuuki, and Ran, and Clovis, and Merida…We all made that promise together, and yet…here I am…"

She seemed to have run out of words. Si-Eun dropped her head, shoulders trembling.

Ran was probably Yuuki's older sister, the original leader of the guild. Which meant the other two unfamiliar names were Sleeping Knights who had already passed away. The fact that they came together by sharing the cruelest of fates seemed to bind them even tighter than family or lovers. Asuna wondered what she could possibly say about something like this, but she couldn't just stay silent.

She reached out with her left hand and engulfed Si-Eun's right as it gripped the edge of the bench. Through her palm, she could feel the thin, bony fingers and their undeniable warmth.

"Si-Eun, I've been thinking lately…that life is a tool to transport and relate the heart. For a long, long time, I was scared. I was scared to tell people my feelings and scared to learn theirs. But Yuuki taught me that you can't think that way. That nothing will come about unless you reach out to touch another. I want to tell many people about the strength Yuuki gave me. For as long as I'm alive, I want to carry Yuuki's heart with me, wherever I go. And… when I see her once again, I want to return all of the heart I've received," Asuna said, carefully, haltingly finding the words as she went. She didn't feel like she'd said even half of what she wanted to, but Si-Eun let her head dip in understanding from its downturned position, and she moved her other hand on top of Asuna's.

When Si-Eun raised her head, her beautiful black eyes were wet with tears, but there was a clear smile on her lips.

"Thank you…Asuna," she whispered, then suddenly held out her arms and circled them around Asuna's back. Asuna embraced her fragile body in return. The words continued at her ear.

"We're all so grateful to you, Asuna. After her sister, Ran, died, Yuuki took her place in cheering us onward and upward. We got so dependent on that…Whenever it was tough or we felt ready to break, we all clung to Yuuki to share in some of her strength. However—and you'll think this is an obvious thing to say—I was worried about her. I wondered who was keeping *her* heart upright. She was always smiling and never let anyone see the pain…but there were so many things resting on that back of hers that it made me afraid her poor heart would collapse under the weight…And that's when you appeared. When you were around, Yuuki was full of so much natural enjoyment and life, it was like watching a little bird that just remembered how to fly again. And she flew higher and higher…until she went to a place…where we can't reach her…"

Si-Eun stopped there for a while. On the screen within her heart, Asuna saw Yuuki for an instant in the shape of a bird, flitting through the foreign skies of an unfamiliar world.

They let go, and Si-Eun smiled bashfully, using a fingertip to brush away her tears. She took a deep breath and clearly, forcefully resumed. "To tell the truth, it's not just me. Jun has…a very tricky form of cancer, but the drug he just started using is working miracles on him, shrinking the tumors. We were talking about it, saying that Yuuki was telling us it wasn't our time to join her yet. It seems like the full reunion of the Sleeping Knights won't be for quite a while."

"…Of course it won't. And you're supposed to be accepting me as an official member next time."

Asuna and Si-Eun shared a look, then a chuckle. Then they looked upward into the pale pink sky. A gentle breeze blew past, rustling their hair. Asuna thought of Yuuki, clutching their shoulders before she beat her wings and flew off into the sky, and closed her eyes.

How many minutes passed? The serene silence was broken by the sound of approaching footsteps. Asuna looked over to see a boy wearing the same color uniform as hers—Kazuto Kirigaya—and Dr. Kurahashi, who was in black mourning garb.

Asuna and Si-Eun stood up together and bowed in greeting. When his own bow was finished, Kazuto said to Asuna, "So this is where you were. Are we intruding?"

"No, it's fine. But…did you always know Dr. Kurahashi, Kirito?"

"Well…only recently. We've been exchanging e-mails about that communication probe."

"That's right," Dr. Kurahashi continued. "That camera really caught my interest. He's been helping me brainstorm how it might be used for medical full-dive purposes."

"Oh, I see. Actually, speaking of which," Asuna said, remembering something, "what will happen to the Medicuboid tests? Is someone else going to take over the monitor…?"

The doctor's cheeks softened in a grin, and he said, "Actually, no, we got more than enough data from the test. The next step is working with the manufacturers to turn it into an actual, viable product. Perhaps Miss Ahn and others like her will be able to use their own Medicuboids soon…"

He said this last part in Si-Eun's direction, then looked shocked when he realized what he was doing. "Oh, pardon me. I really should have said this first: Congratulations on leaving the hospital, Miss Ahn. I'm certain that Yuuki is…very happy about it all…"

Si-Eun took his outstretched hand and shook it. Next, she shook hands with Kazuto, whom she already knew well from the game.

"Thank you. I don't think I'll be allowed to use the Medicuboid anymore…but the thought of Yuuki's data helping others who are fighting disease is…a wonderful thing," she said.

The doctor's head bobbed up and down eagerly. "Yes, indeed. Yuuki's name will remain in history as the first person to test that machine. Along with the external provider of the initial design… she deserves some kind of prestigious award…"

"I don't think that Yuuki would be very excited about something like that. She'd complain that you can't eat it," Si-Eun said.

Everyone laughed. When the pleasant sound subsided, Asuna

realized that something Dr. Kurahashi said was still sticking with her. She asked him, "Doctor...you mentioned an...external provider? Wasn't it the medical appliance manufacturer who designed it?"

"Ahh...w-well," the doctor stammered, his eyes narrowing as he consulted his memory, "the actual creation of the prototype itself was done by the manufacturer, of course. But the base design of the ultra-high-density signal nodes, which is the very heart of the device, was provided pro bono by an outside source. It was a woman...a researcher at a major university overseas. She was Japanese, though. Let's see, her name was..."

The name Dr. Kurahashi mentioned was totally unfamiliar to Asuna. Si-Eun had no reaction, either, but when she glanced over at Kazuto and saw the expression on his face, Asuna's breath caught in her throat.

His gaze was blank, the look of one who couldn't believe what he was seeing. His bloodless lips twitched twice, three times.

"Wh-what's wrong, Kirito?!" she asked, but he did not answer.

Eventually, in a hoarse, cracking voice, he said, "I...I know her."

"Huh...?"

"I've...met her before..."

Kazuto looked into Asuna's eyes. The dark pupils were breaking through the barrier of space-time and staring into a far-off world.

"She's the one who...took care of Heathcliff's body while he was in-dive. She was part of the same research team and studied full-dive capabilities with him...So that means the true provider of the Medicuboid's basic design was..."

"..."

Asuna couldn't find the words, either.

It meant that, just like the Seed Nexus, the Medicuboid was the offshoot of the seeds planted by that enigmatic figure.

Si-Eun and Dr. Kurahashi looked at them in confusion but received no answer. All Asuna could do was follow the path of the cherry blossom petals as they fell before her eyes.

Suddenly, she sensed a great *flow* in the world.

This place we call "reality" was just one individual face.

There was a greater construct made up of many, many worlds, as countless as flower petals.

And a tremendous force that enveloped, shook, and trailed through all the worlds was slowly coming into shape…

Asuna clutched her sides with both hands. A bracing gust of wind picked up the falling petals, carrying them high into the distant sky.

AFTERWORD

Hello, this is Reki Kawahara. Thank you for reading *Sword Art Online 7: Mother's Rosary*. (Please be warned that the following will contain major spoilers for this book!)

Nearly a decade ago, before I seriously began to write, I became acquaintances with a professional novelist and had the opportunity to chat about writing on a number of occasions.

I am still grateful for all of that advice and encouragement, but the strongest memory I have of everything I heard was, "Even in a novel, if you're going to write about someone's misfortune, you have to know exactly why it is that you're writing it."

I will admit that I have a bad habit of ignoring improbability in order to prioritize certain plot developments—some might call it "plot convenience." In particular, I often saddle a character with terrible misfortune in order to provide them direction in terms of personality or motivation. For example, Kirito, the protagonist of the *SAO* series, lost his parents in an accident as a child, but I have not revealed anything about that accident yet. In other words, in order to give Kirito a reason to distance himself from others, I decided to kill off his parents through the statistically improbable traffic accident death. (The same might be said of Sachie, the heroine of the "Red-Nosed Reindeer" story in Volume 2.)

Recognizing that this was a bad writing habit of mine, I decided that when it came time to publish this seventh volume,

I needed to do some rewriting of the original material. This gave me a lot to think about: Just because this book has a theme of VR technology and medical science, does that still mean that Yuuki has to die? Could I have gone with an alternate ending? Was that conclusion nothing more than a cheap attempt at soliciting tears from the reader?

But while I did agonize over these questions, a part of me also believes that a story can only be written in the way it is meant to be. It's absolutely nothing more than an excuse, but my own habit of making light of a character's misfortune is part of the story; in which case, all I can do is think very hard about all of the characters (including villains) who meet with misfortunate events in the story. As long as the readers are able to imagine something of what Yuuki's fifteen years in the world gave to Asuna and the others, I couldn't ask for more.

My heartfelt thanks to my editor, Mr. Miki, who had to deal with my complex and confusing holiday schedule, to my illustrator, abec, for rendering so many new and unfamiliar characters, to my friend Vag for the medical expertise and advice, and of course, to all you readers! Hope you stick with me throughout 2011! Thank you so much!

Reki Kawahara — January 27, 2011